Now & Forever

Now & Forever

SUSANE COLASANTI

VIKING

An Imprint of Penguin Group (USA)

VIKING
Published by the Penguin Group
Penguin Group (USA) LLC
375 Hudson Street
New York, New York 10014

USA * Canada * UK * Ireland * Australia
New Zealand * India * South Africa * China

penguin.com
A Penguin Random House Company

First published in the United States of America by Viking,
an imprint of Penguin Group (USA) LLC, 2014

LIBRARY OF CONGRESS CATALOGING-IN-PUBLICATION DATA
Colasanti, Susane.
Now and forever / by Susane Colasanti.
pages cm
Summary: "When Sterling's boyfriend Ethan's band becomes a YouTube sensation,
she's thrown head-first into the glam world of celebrity"— Provided by publisher.
ISBN 978-0-670-01424-8 (hardcover)
[1. Dating (Social customs)—Fiction. 2. Celebrities—Fiction. 3. Bands (Music)—Fiction.
4. Rock music—Fiction. 5. Self-actualization—Fiction.] I. Title.
PZ7.C6699Now 2014
[Fic]—dc23
2013027005

Printed in the USA   Set in Minion Pro

1   3   5   7   9   10   8   6   4   2

For my readers.
You are all rock stars.

Thank you for making
this life possible.
Much love.

Now & Forever

Prologue

205,132,379.

That's how many times his new video has been viewed. That's how many people went to his site, pressed PLAY, and watched the hottest musician in the world perform his latest single.

It wasn't like this a year ago. No one even knew who he was back then. His website only had a few hundred hits. His music wasn't playing on the radio every five minutes. His music wasn't out there at all. And now it's everywhere.

All these girls' eyes on him. All these strangers singing along in their rooms, on the other side of all those screens all over the world.

He's the world's biggest rock star.

He's the boy every girl wants.

He's my boyfriend.

1

When I open my front door, Ethan is holding his phone over his head playing "In Your Eyes."

"Happy anniversary," he says.

"You remembered!" I've been wondering if Ethan was going to remember that our first date was one month ago today. He didn't say anything at school. So I didn't say anything, either. I didn't want to come off like a total spaz over being together for a month. Now I'm so happy I didn't ruin his surprise. I had no idea Ethan was planning this when he said he wanted to come over tonight.

He comes in and kisses me. Still holding his phone over his head. Still playing "In Your Eyes."

"You rule," I tell him.

"I don't rule yet. Maybe I'll rule when we get to where I'm taking you to celebrate. If you like what we're doing."

"You didn't have to do all this."

Ethan hugs me tight. "I wanted to make tonight special."

It's hard to believe we've only been together for one month. It feels like I've known him forever. Today at lunch we were talking about last Saturday night. We were driving around in Ethan's car with no destination in mind. I was supposed to be home in half an hour. But I was desperately trying to block out the harsh reality of time. So was Ethan.

"What if we kept driving?" Ethan said. "Got a motel room in some random town? We could say we got lost."

"And we got the motel room for safety. You were really tired and we were worried you might fall asleep at the wheel."

"Exactly. Your mom would buy that, right?"

"As much as your mom would."

We smirked at each other. Both moms would see right through that scam.

Ethan reached into my lap and held my hand. This was always the worst part of the night, when we knew we'd have to go home soon. I wanted to drive around all night. Holding hands in my lap or his. Singing along to the radio. Getting lost down side streets to make out. We're both shocked by how much alone time we want together. Neither of us has ever felt this way before. Ethan loves having lots of people around. He's a classic extrovert like me. We're both into going out and meeting new people. But nothing compares to how happy I am when it's just the two of us.

A David Bowie song came on. Ethan started laughing.

"What?" I asked.

"Obscure reference."

"Try me."

"'Hey Bowie, do you have one really funky sequined space suit?'"

"*Flight of the Conchords*! I love that show!"

"How are you so awesome?"

"How are *you* so awesome?"

"We're both *Flight of the Conchords* geeks. That makes us both awesome."

"I love our obscure awesomeness."

"I love everything about you."

Ethan made me melt when he said that. I was melting right into the passenger seat. My bones went soft and my heart swelled and I couldn't imagine ever feeling happier than I did right that second. I knew he could see how much I loved him when he looked into my eyes. We haven't said "I love you" to each other yet. But we both know it's there.

That night in Ethan's car feels like it was three weeks ago. But it was only three days ago. When we're together, time dilates and stretches in mysterious ways. It's like we enter our own private universe. Especially when we're alone.

Especially when we're making out.

When Ethan is touching me and kissing me and we're pressed against each other in bed, I never want it to end. I wish we could stay together forever. We usually go to my apartment after school. One minute it'll be three thirty and we'll have three whole hours until Ethan has to be home for dinner. The next thing we know it's after six. How do hours pass in a space of time that feels like minutes?

I suspect time is going to pass even faster tonight. I have no idea where Ethan's taking me to celebrate. But something tells me it's going to be really romantic.

"In Your Eyes" finishes playing. Ethan smiles in that way he has where his eyes sparkle like I'm the most important person to him.

"Are you ready?" he asks.

Why does it seem like he's asking about more than just tonight?

Ethan won't give me any hints in his car. He even takes a few random turns to fake me out. Our small town is already shut down for the night. The river, piers, and boats all seem like they're sleeping. I'm surprised when we end up at his house.

"Didn't see that coming," I say.

"You have no idea."

No one's home at Ethan's house. We go up to his room. Which is filled with candles. Candles in different shapes, sizes, and colors are on every available surface. Candles are on the windowsills, the dresser, the desk, the shelves, the night table. There are even some big pillar candles clustered in a corner on the floor.

Ethan turns the lights off. He starts lighting candles.

"Have a seat," he says. "This might take a while."

I lie back on Ethan's big bed and watch him light the candles. I love watching him. One time he fell asleep in my room. I watched him for almost an hour, memorizing the slope of his nose, the curves of his cheeks, the shape of his lips.

Ethan Cross is the most gorgeous boy I've ever seen. And he picked me.

How did I get so lucky?

After he lights the last candle, Ethan grabs his iPod. He lies down next to me. Then he puts one earbud in my ear and the other in his.

"Thanks again for the song last night," Ethan says. "I loved it."

I was so nervous about sending Ethan "Everything" by Lifehouse. I've had that song on repeat ever since the day Ethan first asked me out. To me, it's Ethan's theme song. It sounds like him. It feels like him. I love losing myself in the sound of him. I'm so deep in the love haze I can't remember what I used to think about before Ethan. Last night I was suddenly inspired to share the song with him. The message I wrote with it said that he's all I want. He's all I need. What we have is amazing.

The second I sent the song, I worried that it was too much. The last thing I want to do is scare him away. But Ethan isn't a typical boy. He doesn't get freaked out by strong emotions. And he's so romantic.

"Your song inspired me to find one for you," Ethan says. Haunting, resonant music starts playing in our earbuds. "Have you heard of Sigur Rós?"

"No."

"They're Icelandic. They have an ambient, post-rock sound." Ethan strokes my cheek. "Their music is beautiful. Just like you."

Melting. On. The bed.

"I don't have the words to tell you how I feel about you. So I found a song in another language to do it for me. I don't know Icelandic, but I read that it's about two people falling in love. How they spend the day together walking around down-town and enjoying being in their own world where they un-derstand each other better than anyone ever has before. It's called 'An Alright Start.'"

"You always out-romantic me. I thought I was being all sweet sending you 'Everything.' You're like, 'I had to go to a whole other language to tell you how I feel!'"

"You were being sweet. You're the sweetest girl I've ever known."

I put my head on Ethan's chest, breathing with him and listening to the music. Ethan slides his fingers through my hair over and over.

"Sterling," Ethan says.

"Yeah?"

"I love you."

I lift my head to look at Ethan. He glows in the candle-light. Just looking at him takes my breath away.

"I love you, too," I tell him.

How could it be any better than this?

2

"**What key is** this in?" Drew asks.

"B-flat," Gage tells him.

"My pages are messed up." Drew makes some notations on his sheet music with a pencil.

"Let's hit it," Stefan says from behind the drums. Stefan is only happy when he's behind the drums.

Drew, Gage, and Stefan are Ethan's band mates. Those guys' high school days are behind them. Now they're working random jobs while waiting for the band to get megafamous. Their band is The Invincibles. Drew plays bass and Gage rocks the keyboard. Along with Ethan's best friend, Miles, these guys are Ethan's closest friends.

The band breaks into "Now and Forever." Ethan's hoping it will be their first single. He looks at me while he sings.

Don't worry about tomorrow.
We always have today.

Right now is all that matters.
Right now is here to stay.

Ethan wrote this song for me. I couldn't believe he wrote it in two days. He said he was inspired by his muse (i.e. me). "Now and Forever" is all about appreciating the moment you're in, anytime, anywhere. It's about quieting the noisy part of your brain that's anxious about the future and soothing it by finding happiness in whatever you're doing right now. Ethan said that I make him happier than he's ever been. He wanted to write a song that would capture how happy he felt with me.

Yeah. My life is pretty good.

I put my feet up on the edge of the couch cushion, hugging my knees to my chest. Ethan snagged this couch for the garage when his parents redecorated the den. It's perfect for watching band practice.

"That was awesome," Ethan tells the guys when the song ends.

"Did you see 'Aluminum Rain'?" Gage asks Ethan. "I sent it to you last night."

Ethan nods.

"Can we try it?"

Things always get awkward when Gage wants The

Invincibles to play a song he wrote. Everything the band plays was written by Ethan. There's an unspoken understanding that Ethan's music is phenomenal. That's why Ethan is destined to be a rock star.

But Gage thinks he's also destined to be a rock star, despite his music lacking the depth and soul of Ethan's. That's why he keeps pushing Ethan to add his songs to the set list. They've already done some shows at local venues. So far, Ethan's songs are the only ones they've played.

"We don't really have time," Ethan tells Gage.

"Then can we at least add it to the next set list?"

"I don't think that would be the best approach," Ethan says.

"Seriously? Are we ever going to play my songs?"

Ethan glances at the other guys. Drew picks at his bass uncomfortably. Stefan itches to pound the drums.

Gage faces Drew. "You liked 'Aluminum Rain.' You said it spoke to you."

"It's a good song," Drew agrees.

"But not as good as Ethan's songs. Right?"

Drew throws Stefan a look. Stefan looks at his drums.

"Come on, man," Drew says. "Take it easy."

"No, I want to know. That's what you guys really think, right? That Ethan's songs are better than mine. Why don't you just admit it so we can move on?"

"Your songs are good," Stefan says. "Maybe just not as . . . strong."

"We all want to be successful," Drew says. "That's only

going to happen if we rock our strongest sound. You know how hard it is to get people's attention. How long have we been practicing in this garage? Two years? And we only started playing gigs . . . what, three months ago? Things are finally happening for us. We have to stick with what's working."

"You're right." Gage yanks the cover over his keyboard. He grabs his bag.

"Where are you going?" Ethan says. "We still have twenty minutes."

"I'm done."

"You mean . . . for today, or . . . ?"

"I'm not sure this is working for me anymore."

"Dude," Stefan says. "Don't be such a drama queen."

Gage turns to Stefan like he's going to say something. Then he stalks out of the garage to his car. He slams his door and peels out.

"Was it something I said?" Stefan wonders.

Watching band practice is usually fun. These four guys all started out at the same level, practicing in Ethan's garage three days a week after school. The thing is, they're not going to be at the same level for much longer. Especially now that Zeke is in the picture.

Zeke Goldstein is a beast.

Ethan met him at a show they played in New Haven. Zeke wasn't even there scoping out talent. He was on a blind date his friend set up. As soon as Ethan sang his first note, Zeke knew he was destined for greatness. He was determined to sign Ethan

ЁЁЁ

right away. Zeke is on the grind 24/7. He just started working on building Ethan's career and Ethan already has thousands of followers. He says Ethan is about to go places beyond his wildest dreams. And that boy's dreams are pretty wild.

Zeke will be the first one to tell you that he discovered Ethan and that he deserves to take credit for Ethan's future success. Which comes off as arrogant to me. The way Zeke sees it, he's confident in his ability to build an artist's career. And he believes in Ethan more than anyone he's ever represented. He even dropped a few clients to make more room for Ethan on his list. Zeke insists Ethan's career is about to blow up.

"I guess we're done here," Ethan says.

Drew packs his bass. Stefan riffs on the drums.

Ethan comes over and scrunches against me on the couch. "Sorry about the drama," he says.

"Honey badger don't care."

"It just takes what it wants."

"And of course what does the honey badger have to eat for the next two weeks?"

"Cobra!" we both yell.

We were on the floor the first time we saw that video. I don't know what's so hysterical about it. But we were dying. We were also dying over that video of the race car. The race car isn't even moving. It's just a picture of a race car. Some guy is making race-car sound effects over it like, *"Rinnnng neee neee nee nee neeeee!"* Again, way more hysterical than it should be.

Ethan scrunches even closer to me. He holds me tight.

"I have to get up," he says. "But I don't want to get up."

"I don't want you to stop hugging me."

"They need to invent a tool to pry us apart."

He's right. It's like we have to touch each other all the time or we'll die or something. "They should call it the peeler-offer."

"OXO should make one."

"I was just going to say that!" OXO is one of my favorite brands of kitchen tools. They're into form plus function. Which is the best combo for cooking supplies.

Drew and Stefan shuffle over to talk to Ethan before they leave. I go inside. The last thing I want to be is the lead singer's clingy girlfriend.

3

Being a culinary geek means that no shiny new kitchen appliance fails to catch my eye. Or shiny new utensil. Or shiny new tableware. Which is why Crate & Barrel is my mecca.

I'm meeting my best friend, Georgia, for brunch in twenty minutes. The brunch place is across the street. There's no way I could resist coming here first. Not to get anything. There's just something about walking around the kitchen section, admiring how the dazzling light glints off every single glass surface and which spatula colors are the hot trend this season and seeing what new cupcake sprinkles they have, that is incredibly soothing. It makes me happy. And it makes me excited for my future self, who will own most of this stuff.

"May I help you find something?" an employee asks. She has bright red lipstick, a sky-high, gold-streaked ponytail; and enough perky energy to power the entire store.

"No, thanks. I'm just looking."

"For anything in particular?"

"Not really." It's hard to explain what I'm doing here. It's actually kind of embarrassing to try explaining my obsession out loud.

"Let me know if you need anything. I'll be right over there." She points to an island of registers.

"Okay. Thanks." Something sparkly catches my eye behind the registers. I dart over to find out what is so sparkly. Snow-cone cups with neon stripes are stacked in glittering containers. A super profesh snow-cone machine sits next to them along with an array of syrups. The summery display makes me smile. School just ended. I have the whole summer to chill. Cooking and reading are definitely on the agenda. I've recently gotten back into yoga, working on being present in the moment. I want to be more focused, less preoccupied. There will be lots of time to hang out with Georgia and Miles and our other friends. And there will be lots of late nights with Ethan. . . .

A typed sign hanging behind one of the registers says:

DO NOT CLOSE THIS DRAWER. HINGE IS LOSE.

See, that's just depressing. A typo anywhere is insulting. But a typo at Crate & Barrel is personally offensive. I rely on Crate & Barrel to dispense information in their signature smooth, bold font that is both accurate and charmingly lyrical. True, this sign was done by an employee, not corporate. But that's no excuse for ignorance. To bother going to the trouble of typing the sign? And then hanging it where everyone can see?

Ms. Perky swings around behind a register. "Ready to check out?" she asks.

"No, sorry. I was just . . ." There's really no way to explain myself. First with the Crate & Barrel obsession. Now with the typo obsession. I know I'm not normal. But I can't help who I am.

It all started with a vegetable.

My cooking class went to New Haven last year for Restaurant Week. There was a tasting menu at a restaurant where our teacher knew the executive chef. We got to see how they prepped for the dinner rush. When we were walking around earlier that day, we went into a deli for drinks. The deli had an awning that looked brand-new. The awning was green. The awning was huge. And this is what the awning said right across the front:

DELI, GROCERIES, BEER, SNACKS, VEGETABLE

Dude. They only had one vegetable.

I pointed out the typo to a girl from my class. She was like, "We better run in quick and snatch that vegetable up before someone else gets it!"

After the vegetable debacle, I started noticing typos everywhere. On handwritten signs in store windows. At school.

Even on billboards that people had paid a lot of money for. One time when my mom and I were at the grocery store, I saw a handwritten sign on an employees only door that said OPEN "SLOWLY." Those stupid quotation marks annoyed me the whole time I was pushing our cart around. I almost ran over an old lady, I was so annoyed. While Mom was checking out, I went up to the customer service desk.

"How can I help you?" the smiling guy behind the counter said.

"You can actually help everybody. See that sign?" I pointed at the crooked piece of paper on the door.

"Yes?"

"Notice anything strange about it?"

His smile vanished. He looked again.

"What are you getting at?" he accused.

"See those quotation marks around *slowly*?"

"Yes?"

"Why are they there?"

"We've been having problems with the door. People are opening it too fast and slamming into people."

"You don't need those quotation marks," I explained. "The sign should just read 'open slowly.'"

"You serious?" He laughed. "Why are you wasting my time with this?"

I was two seconds away from grabbing the black marker from his desk, marching over to the sign, and scribbling out the quotation marks. But I restrained myself from looking like a lunatic at ShopRite.

"You should correct the sign," I said. Then I walked away. Walking away is not my thing.

For a while after the Open "Slowly" Incident, I corrected any typo I saw on a sign. No sign was safe. I did it on the DL so I wouldn't offend anyone directly. It was my way of trying to make the world a smarter place. But whipping out a marker to change "their" to "there" in "Their are two lanes open" wasn't enough. Not even close.

That's why I want to be a book publisher. The decline of our society's collective intelligence is sad. I mean, really, is this the best we can do? Not that I should talk. I didn't take school seriously up until last year. School was just something I had to endure until I could graduate and focus on real life. But now that I have a career goal I feel passionate about, I'm putting a lot more energy into my classes. I want to show other people that knowledge is a good thing. As a publisher, I'll have the power to share quality work that can change the world. I can make a much greater impact by publishing books that advance our collective intelligence than I can correcting a few random signs three people might notice. My mom is in full support of my career goal. She has a severe dislike for pop culture and what it's doing to our society. She loves that I want to help preserve the English language.

When I see the ridiculous comments posted on Ethan's pages with their typos and misspellings, I want to comment back how stupid they sound. But of course I would never do that. Restraint is just one way I support Ethan's big dream.

4

"Look at this," Ethan says.

Something about being in Ethan's room puts me in a warm, fuzzy trance. Maybe it's how everything is so familiar. Or how it smells like him, a mix of Gucci Guilty and vanilla. I always feel so comfortable here. This is where Ethan grew up. His room knows all his secrets. His true feelings. His desires. I could stay on his bed reading for days. But I pry myself up and go over to his desk. What he's pointing at on the huge computer screen is incredible.

He has 103,204 followers.

"That's over five hundred more than yesterday," he says.

"Of course it is. You're amazing."

Ethan reaches up and pulls me down on his lap. He slides his fingers through my wet hair.

"*You're* amazing," he says.

We just came in from Ethan's pool out back. It's one of the many reasons I love coming over to his house. His house is so massive, you wouldn't even know his parents and little sister live here, too. I've come over lots of times without seeing any of them, even when they're all home.

We read the comments on the new video he posted today. Or Ethan reads while I watch our reflection in the mirror above his desk. I love how good we look together. Ethan is athletic lean with big blue eyes and dark brown hair. He has the kind of look that makes girls melty. I've melted in many locations just because he looked at me in that intense boyfriend way. His eyes are almost the same shade of dark blue as mine. It's weird seeing my hair so dark in the mirror. I changed my hair right before summer vacay. I'm still getting used to it being black with a jade streak.

Ethan pulls me closer. Right when he's about to kiss me, his computer pings with new comments.

How can you look so sexy without even trying? You gangsta now :D

Hot video. Scorching. En fuego.

OMG!!!!!! we luv u in richmond, Ethan! Do a show hre pleeeeeze???

The very first comments Ethan got when he started posting videos two years ago were exciting. He told me he used to write everyone back. That was before I knew him. It's so weird how I didn't even talk to him back then. Ethan still reads and appreciates every comment, but now there are way too many for him to write back to everyone. He would if he could, though. The boy has serious love for his fans.

This new video is getting more views and comments than ever. Ethan's mom hired a professional filmmaker to do his last three videos. Then Ethan hooked up with Red Bedroom Records, an indie label that's all about discovering stellar new talent. He recorded his first album with them. *Forever* is about to drop. Red Bedroom only wanted Ethan, so he recorded *Forever* without The Invincibles. He's hoping that attention for the album will inspire attention for the band. Ethan's stoked that Zeke signed him in the spring. That gave Zeke time to hustle enough to make sure *Forever* will be huge.

Red Bedroom is releasing the song for this video, "Night on Fire," as Ethan's first single off the album. The video is fierce. Instead of the standard overproduced video format, Ethan wanted to go with something more relatable to his fans. He filmed most of the video himself with a handheld camera. The filmmaker recorded the longer shots of Ethan and did the editing. "Night on Fire" is about one magical summer night when a boy and girl meet. They have this immediate connection. It's love at first sight. In the video, they spend the whole night together in downtown Manhattan, playing mini golf on a pier in Tribeca, getting Italian ices at Rocco's, and walking along the Hudson River. He kisses her on the rooftop of a building they sneak into, sparkles of city lights all around them. Watching the sunrise, they realize that no matter what happens, they will always have this one night to remember forever. The fire of their passion will never die.

Obviously, this video is speaking to a lot of girls. More melting the first time I saw it.

Ethan isn't a typical teen rock star. His music has a quality and depth that boy bands typically lack. You can totally hear Ethan's influences in his music. His sound is a combination of pop and hip-hop mostly inspired by The Beatles, Elvis, and Michael Jackson. Ethan believes they were the musicians who made music what it is today. He's also into contemporary artists like Eminem, Usher, and Justin Timberlake. Ethan's musical style is hard to describe. He has a unique sound no one else has ever created before. Even though his music is so original, its tone is familiar. His songs somehow relate to everyone. They just feel like home. His lyrics achieve the impossible by being both catchy and deep. His target demographic is girls ages twelve to twenty-four. But nine-year-old girls and grandmas also love him. Plus he has lots of guy fans. Basically, Ethan makes the kind of music generations have been waiting for. It's obvious why he has such widespread appeal.

More comments pop up.

Brazil LOVES YOU!!! Te amo xxx

Where can I get a night on fire?

Ahhhhh how are you so perfect? <3

"That last comment was obviously meant for you," Ethan tells me.

"You're the one who's perfect. I should know. I'm your biggest fan."

"Hmm." Ethan scans the comments. "I wonder why my biggest fan didn't comment?"

"All of my comments are private."

"But you like the video, right?"

"I love it. You're so hot I can't believe the screen didn't ignite."

Ethan kisses me. When Ethan kisses me, every part of me ignites.

"Ahem," goes a voice in the doorway.

"Nice knock," Ethan says.

"Um, your door was open?" Sydney says with tone. Sydney is Ethan's little sister. She is thirteen and not at all impressed with Ethan. Which is ironic considering she's in his target demographic. If Ethan becomes even half as famous as he's hoping, Sydney's friends will be dying that he's her brother.

"What can I do for you?" Ethan asks.

"Mom wants to know where Sterling put the garlic press."

"Then why don't you ask her?"

Sydney's detached gaze flicks over to me. I'm still sitting on Ethan's lap. She's clearly wondering why I'm even remotely interested in her brother.

"It's in the second drawer by the refrigerator," I tell her. "The one with the big utensils."

"That's not where it goes."

"Oh, sorry. I thought it was."

Sydney retreats, shaking her head at the floor over my audacity at presuming to shove a garlic press where it does not belong. She plods downstairs to rectify my outlandish behavior.

"How dare you," Ethan says.

"I thought that's where it went."

"Garlic presses don't like to be misplaced."

"Oh, really?"

"Know what happens to people who put garlic presses in the wrong drawer?"

"What?"

"Tickling."

"No tickling."

Ethan presses his fingers against my sides.

"No tickling!" I spring up from his lap, laughing hysterically even though the tickling never started. Even the threat of tickling makes me hyper.

More pings from Ethan's computer. More comments from girls all over the world raving about how cute and sexy and talented he is. Ethan scrolls down to read the new ones.

I want to stay in Ethan's room forever. Every time I leave, it feels like I'm leaving part of myself behind. Tonight, with the summer breeze drifting in the windows and the smell of dinner cooking downstairs and senior year about to start, I'm overcome by warm contentment.

I guess I'm just feeling nostalgic tonight. But also excited about the possibility of Ethan becoming a huge rock star. He's worked so hard for this. How much time has Ethan spent in his room, in the garage practicing with his band, in jam sessions, in studios, building the dream? Enough for this to be his time.

Something tells me that the way we are right now at the end of summer, on the edge of everything, is a way we will never be again.

Something tells me our whole world is about to change.

5

I breeze by the nurses' station with my brightly colored bunch of balloons, waving to one of the nurses I know. I make sure the tissue paper sticking out of the gift bag I'm carrying isn't crushed. Then I go in.

"Hi, Gram!"

My grandma smiles when she sees me. She always smiles when she sees me.

"There's my girl," she says from her bed by the windows. She was originally assigned the other bed by the door. But when I was pushing her wheelchair here from the recovery room after her heart surgery and saw that both beds were empty, I asked one of the nurses if we could take the other bed. I am so relieved she let us. This part of the room is much better. Not only does it have sunlight and views, it's large enough for a reclining chair. A reclining chair I've been camping out in every day since Gram's surgery.

"What's all this?" Gram gestures to the gifts.

"Your balloons needed refreshing." The bunch of three "get well soon" balloons I tied to her bed rail the first day I visited is floating halfway down. I untie them and tie the new bunch where they were. Then I bring the gift bag over to Gram.

She gestures at the bed's control panel. This means she wants me to raise the bed so she can sit up. When we get the bed the way she wants, she looks at the gift bag.

"You shouldn't have spent your money on me," she says. She says this about everything. Even if you try to give her a paper clip, she will insist she is unworthy.

"I didn't. It's Mom's money."

"Oh, well. That's different," Gram jokes. Her hands are shaky as she takes the bag. She lifts out the sparkly blue tissue paper and reaches inside.

"It's just something little."

Gram takes out a deck of cards. They have pictures of Elvis on the back.

"Elvis!" she raves. Gram is a huge Elvis fan. She's convinced he's still alive somewhere, enjoying his peanut butter and banana sandwiches in a remote hideaway.

"Do you want to play?"

"Absolutely."

I wheel over her bed tray. Then I sit on the side of her bed and rip the plastic wrap off the cards.

"Rummy 500?" I ask.

"What else?"

Rummy 500 is our game. We've been playing it since I was little, way back when Gramp was still alive. I shuffle the cards in the fancy way he taught me: dividing the deck in two, shuffling them down, then back up in a bridge. Gram grabs the pad and pencil on her nightstand to keep score.

"How's Ethan?" Gram asks.

"Awesome. His first single is being released next week."

"That 'Night on Fire' one?"

I nod, placing the pile of cards on the table for Gram to cut the deck. Gram adores Ethan. She knows all his songs, all his videos. She's a major fan.

"That boy is going to be famous," she proclaims.

"I know."

"No. I mean, *really* famous."

The way Gram says it, you have to believe her.

"Did Mom visit yesterday?" I deal the cards.

"She didn't get a chance. She's always busy, that one. Running . . . doing . . ." Gram fans out her hand of cards, trying to space them evenly.

Mom should have visited Gram before she left on another business trip. She should be here right now. With both of us. But I don't say anything.

"Your mother works very hard," Gram says. "She works very hard to give you everything you need."

"I know."

"Just because she can't always be here doesn't mean she loves you any less."

Gram is totally right. It's not like I'm being neglected or anything. Plus I'm leaving for college soon. It really doesn't matter anymore. I used to be super lonely. Even with having friends over all the time and my yoga and cooking classes and activities over the years, those nights when Mom was away on business trips felt so empty. Gram would come over to keep me company and spend the night. She lives down the street. But she hasn't been feeling well, so she doesn't come over as much anymore. Ethan is usually over if my friends aren't. It's not that I'm alone. It's just that sometimes it's lonely without Mom around.

But that's okay. Who wants their parents around all the time? Having my friends and Ethan over whenever I want is awesome. And being strong and independent like Gram is badass. Gram has always been there for me. She's the only one in my family whom I can count on. Which is why it's so important for me to be here for her.

"I still can't get over your hair," Gram says.

The color was so dark when I dyed it black. I thought it needed something to break up the darkness. That's why I had the jade streak put in a little while after. My natural color is light brown. It's never really worked for me. Even when I tried a purple streak in it for a while last year. The first time I dyed my hair was the summer before tenth grade. I wanted it to come out a pretty blonde like my friend Marisa's. But the blonde I ended up with wasn't pretty. I dyed it back to brown that April.

Gram reaches for my jade streak. I lean forward so she can touch it. "It's so soft," she says. "I remember when my hair was soft like that."

The part of Gram's oxygen tube that goes into her nose is sticking out on one side. I reach over and gently press it back in.

"Thank you," she says. She quickly looks back down at her cards. But not before I see her eyes fill with tears.

Gram hates being like this. She doesn't like having to rely on anyone to take care of her. Taking care of people is her thing. She's been a strong, independent woman her whole life. But for a few months leading up to her angioplasty and now in the hospital recovering, a lot of her freedom has been snatched away. Depending on other people to help her with the simplest things is killing her. I can't think about what this is doing to her. If I think about it, I will start bawling and will never be able to stop.

So I stay strong. Or I try to. I visit Gram every day. I make sure she has everything she needs. I try to make her room look as cheerful as possible. Fresh balloons. The floral bedspread I brought from her house. A bouquet of roses that's barely masking the smell of hospital disinfectant. At least they're pretty to look at.

Appearances can make a huge difference. Making Gram's hospital room more comfortable is the only thing about her situation I can control. I keep hoping that if everything looks happy on the outside, maybe the rest will be okay.

6

The Invincibles have a show tonight at The Space, this all-ages venue near New Haven. They've played a bunch of local venues over the past three years. This is the biggest one. The Space printed huge posters with THE INVINCIBLES all big as the headliner. The posters are everywhere—out in front of The Space, on parking meters, in café windows. It's so freaking exciting.

We got here this afternoon for sound check. Then Ethan and I spent a few hours walking around New Haven. We've both been here a bunch of times. New Haven is our closest city. I like seeing all the familiar places again. The yoga shop where I got my yoga mat. The Italian district with the best pizza. The toy store where Ethan kissed me next to the finger paint. The boy is so hot he can even make me melt in a toy store.

I wanted to get back to The Space early to scope out the scene. The crowd is usually just Yale students and locals. But it seems like everyone is here tonight. A few kids from school are even here. The Invincibles go on in half an hour. It's hard to believe Ethan was playing to an empty room at this random arts center three years ago and tonight he's headlining at a packed club.

Sunset Victim is the opening act. The crowd is way into them. Which is impressive, considering that almost everyone is here for Ethan. They're a cool band for being older. Their lead singer/guitarist sounds a lot like Morrissey from The Smiths. He has a sweet emo vibe with his shabby-chic tie and ratty Converses. The bassist is rocking a teal theme. His pants, shoelaces, watch, and earplugs are all teal. I wonder why he has to wear earplugs. Maybe that's what happens when you're over thirty and still in a band.

Georgia wanted to come tonight. She had to go to her cousin's wedding. I wish she were here. I could really use my best friend to help me chill. Ethan and the guys are backstage getting ready while I'm trying to blend in with the crowd. But blending in is hard to do when no one else is alone.

"Are you a Sunset Victim fan?" a girl yells to me over the music. She's wearing horn-rimmed glasses, a tee that says INITECH, and looks like she's in her midtwenties.

"Not really. I mean, they rock, but I'm here for Ethan Cross. How about you?"

"I work with Wade. The guy on bass?"

"Oh, cool. His color coordination is impressive."

"I'll pass along the compliment."

"Do you work in the music industry?"

"No, we're programmers. You'd be surprised how many tech geeks are wannabe rock stars."

We watch Sunset Victim start a new song. This time, the girl on keys sings the lead. They're good. Like, *really* good. Hearing hot bands that are unknown despite their tremendous talent makes me realize how hard it is to break out. How many awesome bands are there in the world? How many bands stay together for five, ten, even twenty years, refusing to give up on the dream? The fact that so many bands like Sunset Victim exist makes it even more amazing that Ethan is finally blowing up.

"So you're a big Ethan Cross fan, huh?" the girl asks.

"I'm his biggest fan."

"Don't all fans say that?"

"Yeah, but in my case it's true."

"Prove it."

"Let's go."

"Where?"

"You'll see."

We push our way through the crowd. Ethan showed me the side door that leads backstage when we were here for sound check. He said I should tell the guy guarding the door that I'm on the list.

"You on the list?" the door guard wants to know.

"Yes. I'm Sterling—that's me." I point to my name on his

list. The glare he gives me makes it clear that this guy does not appreciate people poking at his clipboard. I'm just so excited that my name is on a backstage access list. How cool is that?

He opens the door for us.

"Thanks," we say.

"Enjoy."

We go down a dim, narrow hallway to the dressing rooms. I try to ignore the scribbled sign on one of the dressing room doors marked PRIVITE. The marker in my bag itches to be set free. But I don't want to look like a dork at Ethan's biggest show ever.

"Um . . . how did we get backstage?" the girl asks.

"You'll see."

Ethan is in the last dressing room. The door is open. He likes leaving his dressing room door open so people can feel free to drop in. Ethan is getting pumped, tossing a foam football around with the band guys, who are lounging on the couch.

"Hey, baby." Ethan comes over and gives me a big hug. I can feel his heart hammering with adrenaline. He gets nervous before every show.

"Hey. It's packed out there."

"I saw."

"Some kids from school came."

"Who?"

"I think they're sophomores." I reluctantly pull away from

him. "Ethan, this is . . . Sorry, I don't think I asked what your name is."

The girl is staring at Ethan. "Holy crap." She bugs her eyes out at me, mouth hanging open. "You're Ethan's girlfriend?"

"Told you I was his biggest fan."

"Holy crap." The girl is incapable of elaborating. And I still don't know her name.

The stage manager knocks on the open door. "Ten minutes," he says.

Ethan goes over to his bag and looks for something. I know it's the *mati* his grandfather gave him after his fifth-grade talent show. A *mati* is an eye symbol that protects against negative energy. His grandfather was given this *mati* in Santorini when he was little. The old man who gave him the *mati* had survived cancer and many years of poverty, and outlived his entire family. Now it's Ethan's good-luck charm. He puts it in his pocket before every show.

"We should let you get ready." I kiss Ethan on the cheek. I'm not a shy girl, but something about kissing Ethan on the lips in front of the band is awkward. Sometimes the guys watch us instead of looking away. "I'll be right up front," I tell him, taking my camera out of my bag. Ethan wanted me to take pictures tonight for his fan page.

"Thanks for doing this," Ethan says.

"No thanks needed. When you're the most famous rock star in the world, you can thank me then."

The guys laugh. But I know what Ethan's thinking. He

wants to be that rock star so badly it hurts. He can feel it. He can taste it.

Ethan knew he was going to be famous when he was six. That's when he started taking guitar and voice lessons. He told me about that day he was at a guitar lesson. He was strumming a new chord when he suddenly knew he was meant for insane fame. He was too young to understand the scope of his epiphany, but he knew in his heart what it meant. His fate was undeniable.

He was *six*.

Ever since then, Ethan's been working hard to turn his big dreams into reality. His philosophy is that if you have a strong vision of what you want and you do something every day to work toward that goal, you will eventually achieve it.

As the guys laugh at the possibility of backing up the world's biggest rock star, I wonder if that's exactly who Ethan will become.

7

"I hate that I missed it!" Georgia wails.

"Your cousin got married. I think that's a *bit* more important than a show."

"As if it was just any show." Georgia shakes her head miserably at the orange bell peppers she's chopping. We're making a big, fresh salad in my kitchen. We have the apartment to ourselves. As usual. "I should have been there."

"You'll be there next time. And it'll be even better. Trust me, Ethan is blowing up." Ethan was amazing last night. The Space crowd was electric. When he came onstage, girls screamed so loudly my eardrums buzzed. They were fangirling hardcore the whole show. They couldn't get enough.

"I was reading comments after the show. Your pictures were fabulous."

"Thanks. But we can do better. I'm thinking of asking Marisa to take pictures at the next show."

"You should. Her pics are mad profesh. She could seriously sell them."

"Zeke has been talking about setting up a merchandise page on Ethan's website. Maybe he'll post some there if she takes them."

"Girls will be on them faster than you can say 'door poster.'"

Looking at Georgia sitting across the kitchen counter, it hits me how funny time is. How funny and weird and bittersweet. Two years ago, Marisa was the one sitting there. She was my best friend. And now Georgia is.

Georgia moved here at the beginning of last year. I reached out to her in Earth Science to make her feel welcome. Being the new girl at a small school must have been excruciating. I wanted her to know that I had her back from the start. We both had lunch after class. I asked if Georgia wanted to sit at my table.

"Oh my god *thank you*," she said. "I was up all night worrying about sitting alone. You totally saved me."

We instantly bonded over Rachael Ray.

"I *love* her," I gushed when Georgia took a Rachael Ray collapsible sandwich box out of her lunch bag.

"She's so talented," Georgia agreed. "And cute. And funny. How is that fair?"

"I think it's inspiring. She proves that you can have it all."

"She makes a seriously delicious cookie." Georgia took out something wrapped in aluminum foil. She opened the foil to reveal four of the most appetizing chocolate chip cookies I'd ever seen. They looked almost as good as mine.

"Did your mom make those?" I asked.

"No, I did. I love to bake."

"So do I!"

"That's so cool. How did you get into cooking?"

"My mom can't cook. I took over the kitchen when I was twelve. I even take cooking classes."

"There's a cooking class? I didn't know that."

"It's an outside class. You could still sign up if you want. It just started."

Georgia joined my cooking class. Then she showed me how she tweaked Rachael Ray's chocolate chip cookie recipe to make it even better. We've been inseparable ever since.

"Should I mix a dressing?" Georgia asks when the big salad is done. We never use bottled dressing. Bottled dressing is for amateurs.

"Sure."

"What do you feel like?"

"Something tangy. Spicy mustard, maybe?"

"Done." Georgia springs off the stool and comes around the counter to dig through the refrigerator. Mom always keeps it stocked with whatever I want. I make a grocery list for her every week. We usually go grocery shopping together when she's around on weekends. It's our thing.

"You're running low on spicy mustard," Georgia announces, her head in the refrigerator. "How about something with orange?"

"Oooh, Jamie Oliver does a sage and orange dressing you'd love."

"We have liftoff!"

I love that Georgia gets as excited about cooking as I do.

We take our salads over to the couch. My laptop is waiting on the coffee table. We look at pictures from last night again. Tons of comments are still coming in.

> Could you possibly be more gorgeous? Love everything about this pic—the lights, the angle. Great shot.

> Ethan, your music is elevating the industry standard at a time when music that means something is rarely being produced. Thank you for the enlightenment.

> ur sooooo cute!!!!!

There's been a huge spike in Ethan's followers since yesterday. Could that have been from the show? I check his fan page. Someone posted a video from the show that already has over ten thousand views.

We go to his website. The "Night on Fire" video has a lot more comments. Even his older videos are getting way more comments now.

"Wow," Georgia marvels, "Ethan's a freaking rock star."

"Look at this." I point at the most depressing comment on the "Night on Fire" video:

> awsome u look so hottt ur my fav musisan I wnt 2
> met u on day lv jen age 11

"Does anyone know how to spell anymore?" Georgia says.

"It's a dwindling skill. Beyond depressing. It should not be hard for people to spell words correctly. Hot with three Ts? How pathetic is it when misspelled words are actually longer than the correct spelling?"

"Maybe this new generation is a group of aliens who've come to Earth to abduct our intelligence."

"Wouldn't it be hilarious if I could edit Ethan's comments? These fangirls wouldn't even know how to read them."

Georgia looks at me. "It really bothers you."

"Of course it does! These girls are making themselves look like idiots. Is that the best they can do?"

"Why does it bother you so much?"

"You know my relationship with typos is volatile."

"Oh, I know. But there's not much we can do about the fangirls. That's how they write."

"You're right. I should chill. He has plenty of smart fans. Some of these comments are clearly from Yale students."

"And teachers and doctors and PhD candidates. Everyone loves Ethan."

It's astounding how widespread Ethan's appeal is. Which is exactly what he needs to blow up even more. After all of his dreaming and hoping and hard work, his time is finally here. Typos and all.

8

Oh my god.

Ethan's first single is on the radio.

Shut. UP.

I'm so excited I can hardly work my phone to call him.

"Hey," Ethan answers like nothing's going on. Like the moment we've been waiting for isn't happening *right this very second*.

"So I guess you're not listening to Z100."

"Why?"

"Why do you think?"

"It's on?!" I hear Ethan turn on his radio. Both our radios have been set to Z100 for any Invincibles news. It's basically all I've been playing for the past two weeks. I turned my radio on the second I got home from school today. "I thought it wasn't coming on until tomorrow."

"You're on the radio, baby!"

"Holy shit."

We're quiet for a few seconds, listening to "Night on Fire" fill our rooms. I imagine all of the other rooms it's playing in. All of the people hearing Ethan for the first time. All of his fans who've been waiting for this moment right along with us.

"This is it," Ethan says with a shaky laugh.

"This is it," I confirm.

"We have to celebrate. I'll pick you up in ten."

I dash to my computer to check Ethan's fan page. Comments are popping up like crazy.

> You are on Z100 right now, Ethan Cross! You sound amazing! Congrats!!

> girl you got me wired 3am not even tired there will never be another night on fire

> Welcome to the big time, baller. Don't stop never stop.

By the time Ethan rings my bell, I'm so excited for him that I'm actually trembling. He's smiling all big when I open the door.

"Hello, rock star," I coo.

Ethan swoops in, picks me up, and twirls me around in one smooth motion. His arms are even more ripped than they were last week. He's getting crazy strong now that he's working out six days a week. He's doing three days of cardio or hip-hop dance, two days of weight training, and one day of running or other outdoor activities. And he has pickup basketball games with friends in his limited free time.

"Working out much?" I say.

"Not enough." Ethan gently puts me down. He kisses me. Then he keeps kissing me.

"I thought we were going out to celebrate," I remind him.

"This is celebrating." Ethan slides his hands under my shirt.

"My mom's going to be home any minute."

"What? Why?"

"Um, she lives here?"

"How dare she." Ethan kisses me one last time. "Are you in a Notch mood?"

The Notch is like the only place to hang out around here. It's a mall with a bunch of standard stores, plus a movie theater and bowling alley. Lately we've been hanging out there at Shake Shack. It's the closest we can get to a social scene without driving half an hour to New Haven.

"That's the best you can come up with?" I tease. "You're on the freaking *radio*. How long have you been waiting for this?"

"I know, but I can't bail on training. There's no time to drive to New Haven."

"Then let's hit Shake Shack."

Ethan checks his watch. "Yeah, that'll work. I need carbs."

There are all these rules about what Ethan can eat when.

He's been doing five small meals a day. He has to have carbs an hour and a half before cardio for energy. He has to do a protein shake twenty minutes after lifting, to help build muscle mass. Sometimes I'll make his breakfast, lunch, and snack the night before and give him a big bag with everything before school. Cooking for him makes me happy.

When we get to the Notch, I can feel a difference. Nothing is different specifically. It's more like . . . the air is charged in a way it never has been before. Girls have always looked at Ethan. He gets noticed wherever we go. But now it seems like everyone is noticing him. Even, like, dads. You can feel people turn their heads to watch Ethan when we walk by. Maybe it's that he's more confident now with his first single out. Or maybe people are starting to know who he is outside of school.

We go to Shake Shack. I get my usual: portobello burger, cheese fries, and a large strawberry lemonade. Ethan gets the same, minus the cheese on his fries. Then he changes his mind about the strawberry lemonade. He orders a small Diet Coke and a water.

"You never get the portobello burger," I say. We put our trays down at a corner booth.

"My trainer wants me off red meat."

"And what's with the Diet Coke? Since when do you drink diet anything?"

"Since my trainer threw down calorie restrictions. Remember that chart I showed you?"

I stab a cheese fry with the little wooden spear. Whenever

Ethan talks about his trainer, it makes me feel bad about anything I eat in front of him that isn't broccoli.

Ethan smiles at me. "How can such a tiny, cute girl eat like
you and stay so tiny and cute?"

He's kind of right about the tiny part. My doctor says I
have a high metabolism. But the cute part? I've seen at least a
hundred girls who are knockouts post photos of themselves
on Ethan's page. Will he still think I'm cute after seeing hundreds more?

"Yo, Ethan!" some football player from school yells from
the other side of Shake Shack. "Heard you on the radio! Nice
one, man!"

Ethan gives him an air pound. Air pounding is Ethan's
new thing.

"So Gram's back from the hospital," I say.

Ethan's face lights up. "That's awesome! How is she feeling?"

"Better. Sort of. It's hard to tell with her. She never really
says when she's not feeling well. She'd rather hide it than
bother someone. Not that it's even bothering—"

"Can I get you anything else?" A waitress who looks a
few years older than us is hovering by our table. Hovering by
Ethan.

"No, we're good." He flashes her the stellar Ethan Cross
smile that makes girls melt. This girl is no exception.

"Okay . . . well . . . just let me know if you need anything."

"Will do."

I stab three cheese fries together.

"You were saying?" Ethan reminds me.

"What? Oh, just that I think Gram's feeling better." Could this waitress be any more obvious? First off, the only time they ever come out to the tables here normally is to clean up. You order at the counter. Which is also where you get your food when it's ready. There was no reason for her to come over here. Other than to try to make Ethan notice her. Did she even notice *me*?

It's hard to swallow my fries. They almost get stuck in my throat. I start coughing and grab at my lemonade.

"You okay?"

I take big gulps of lemonade. *Get a grip, Sterling. This is only the beginning.*

"Some VIP service, huh?" Ethan gestures to the waitress. She's back behind the counter, but she keeps looking over here.

"Better get used to it."

"I can't stand that stuff. Like when celebs walk into some restaurant and if they don't get the best table they're all, 'Do you know who I am?' It's like, 'Yeah, you're a pretentious bitch, sit the fuck down.'"

I laugh. Celebs can be so obnoxious. Even the ones who were nice before they were famous. Why do they get like that? Just because everyone knows who they are? How does that entitle them to treat people like dirt? No matter how famous Ethan gets, he would never be rude to anyone.

"So what's going on with you?" I ask. "It feels like I haven't seen you in forever." Between Ethan's insane workout schedule, dance practice, and everything he's doing to launch his career, I'm lucky if I get to see him more than twice a week outside of school.

"Sorry about that." Ethan reaches across the table to cover my hand with his. "Zeke set up all these interviews and promo for the album. I can't believe it drops in two weeks."

"Then your dad will finally have to admit you're not wasting your time."

"Don't bet on it. He was fighting with my mom again last night. He's pissed that she keeps—and I quote—'enabling those silly rock star fantasies.' Like he can force her to stop helping me out. It's her money, too."

Ethan's mom is incredibly supportive of his dreams. But sometimes it seems like all Ethan cares about is winning the approval of his dad. His dad never spends time with Ethan. He's always working. When he is home, he's the first one to tell Ethan that he should be spending more time on school and less time on music. It's probably part of the reason Ethan craves the attention that comes with insane fame. He's not getting it at home from the person he wants it from the most.

"How can he keep being so oblivious when your single's on the radio and your album's about to drop? It's like he *wants* to be in denial." I'm quivering with sympathy for Ethan.

"He doesn't care. You know what he said when I told him about all the interviews I'm doing? 'It's great that things are going well for you now. But what's your plan for the future?'"

"He did *not* say that."

"Totally said it."

"He has no idea how huge you're going to be. Watch when you get a million followers. He'll be begging you to forgive him."

"That's not the only drama. Zeke wants to change the band's name from The Invincibles to Ethan Cross and The Invincibles."

"Why?"

"I think he's trying to phase the guys out. Not phase them out, but eventually he just wants to call us 'Ethan Cross.' He said the band members are irrelevant. He said I'm the one people are coming to see. Which makes sense. *Forever* has my name on it, not the band's."

"Wow. Do the guys know?"

"Oh, yeah. Gage is furious. Drew and Stefan said it was okay, but I can tell they're not happy, either."

"I don't blame them."

"You don't agree with Zeke?"

"No, I do, but . . . I mean, of course he's right. But to put it out there like that is kind of harsh."

"Reality is harsh sometimes. It's not like the guys won't be in the band anymore."

I can't believe Ethan's being like this. It's like he doesn't even feel bad for those guys. We haven't really disagreed on anything. But this feels like it could escalate into our first fight if we keep talking about it.

I stab another cheese fry.

Ethan looks at his watch. "We have to go soon."

"Already? We just got here."

"I know. But I can't be late for training."

My stomach fills with hollow shakiness. Today should have been epic. We've been waiting to hear Ethan's first single on the radio for so long. But sitting here with him has just felt empty. The cute moments and inside jokes we always share were missing. Ethan seems preoccupied, like he's carving out time to see me from his busy schedule. A schedule packed with priorities that are more important than me. I used to be the most important thing in Ethan's life. I don't feel that certainty anymore.

I must look as crushed as I feel because Ethan comes over to my side of the booth. He slides in and puts his arm around me. "Things will calm down after *Forever* drops. I have to tear this publicity stuff up like a beast to get enough buzz going. But we'll get back to normal soon." He gives me a sweet kiss on the cheek. "I promise."

9

"We are gathered here today to say goodbye to a spirit that will be missed," Georgia intones. We're having a plant funeral in her backyard. Her beloved ponytail palm succumbed to aphids. It wasn't pretty.

Georgia loves plants. Her room is filled with them. She gets most of them from the farmers market. Even though she has way more plants than she probably should, when a potential new plant calls out to her, she has to adopt it. Or "him," as she would say. That's how it was with the ponytail palm. She was considering a more mature ponytail palm. But this scraggly little guy called out, "Pick me!" She wanted to give him a chance. Just like Charlie Brown did with that runt of a Christmas tree. She had to take him home.

Being scraggly wasn't his only challenge. He must have been suffering from an aphid attack that Georgia didn't notice when she was first smitten with him. She saw the fuzzy white bugs on him a few days later. No one knows where they come from. They were probably on the plant when she bought him. Or they could have been in the soil Georgia used to repot him. They could have even been in the air. That's how they travel from plant to plant.

Georgia flew into a panic. She was freaking out that all her plants were going down. She fretted over everyone, spraying them with plant bug killer. She waited. Then she sprayed some more. All of her spraying paid off. The ponytail palm was the only casualty of the infestation.

You have to be careful about who you bring home.

We look down at the trashed ponytail palm at the edge of the woods. He had such promise.

"Although he only cost three dollars, the joy this ponytail palm brought to my room was unquantifiable." Georgia peers at me with faux somberness. "Care to add anything?"

"No, I'm good."

"Then tell me what's happening with Ethan's website," Georgia says, walking back toward her house. "I couldn't get on last time I tried."

"It crashed right after 'Night on Fire' was released. It was down for a few hours."

"That's awesome!"

"How is that awesome?" When "Night on Fire" aired two days ago, Ethan's website was mobbed with a deluge of hits.

Not being able to get on might have made a lot of people forget to try going back later.

"People are into the song." Georgia holds her back door open for me. "It's getting crazy. Did you see how many followers he has now?"

"Yeah." Almost a million. Almost one million people know about Ethan. No. Way more people know about him than that. Almost one million people like him enough to follow him. Which means *millions* of people know who Ethan Cross is.

The first thing Georgia does when we get to her room is check her plants to confirm they're aphid-free. I crash on the corduroy pouf. I love Georgia's room. It has a rustic, arts and crafts feel. Big curtains with cross-stitched flowers. A tree trunk for a night table. An ancient credenza with a stubborn door that's determined to remain crooked. My favorite thing in here is Georgia's dark wooden desk. It's super old and looks like it might collapse if you drop a book on it too hard. Her mom found it at a garage sale after they moved here. My room is more sparkly and polished. I like when everything is where it's supposed to be. Georgia only cleans her room when her mom makes her.

"How do they look?" Georgia asks. She'll never stop worrying about her plants.

"Free and clear. That was a close one."

Georgia's phone buzzes on her desk, rattling the compass sitting next to it. Georgia has been taking a compass with her on hikes ever since she saw *127 Hours*.

She checks her phone. "Of course," she grumbles.

"What?"

"A text from Kurt. He said he can't go to the drive-in. He already has plans Saturday night."

"Bummer." A bunch of us are going to the drive-in. It's this vintage outdoor movie theater that was renovated a few years ago. The plan is to do dinner first, then pile into a few cars for the drive-in. Georgia asked if Kurt wanted to go as a group thing. She's been crushing on him since this summer when they both worked at Happy Mart. He usually had the shift after hers. She'd find excuses to stay late and talk to him. Georgia was getting the feeling that he liked her. I guess the group dynamic wasn't casual enough for him. Or maybe he really does have plans.

Georgia flops on her bed, staring at her phone like she's willing the letters of Kurt's text to rearrange themselves into a happier message.

"We could go another night," I suggest. "I'm sure everyone won't mind rescheduling. What about Friday?"

"So I can ask Kurt to go out Friday and watch him reject me again? I'll pass."

"We don't know if he rejected you. He probably has plans like he said."

"Then why didn't he offer another night to go out?"

"Because you asked him to come with us to the drive-in. If you asked him to hang out whenever, that would have been different."

"I should have done that first. Then if he said he wanted

to, I should have asked about the drive-in. I am *such* an idiot."

"No, you're not. It was better to ask him to do a group thing. That way you could feel him out."

"I won't be feeling any part of him now." She glares at her phone. "Why did I break up with Andy again?"

"He's too far away."

"Yeah," Georgia sighs wistfully. "Too far."

Andy was Georgia's boyfriend at her old school. She broke up with him before she moved. She said that a long-distance relationship between Connecticut and Oregon would never work. I have to agree with her. How can you have a relationship with someone you never see in person?

Not that I'm a relationship expert or anything. I used to only talk to boys online. I got a harsh wake-up call in tenth grade when I went to meet someone who said he was an older guy, but who turned out to be the freshman who played the triangle in band. Triangle Boy Incident was a reality check. Anonymous online connections can never lead to something real. Neither can being so distant from your boyfriend that he becomes just a voice on the phone.

I hate that Georgia is going through this. Except for Ethan, most people I know are having a bad week. There's like this negative energy in the air. As if all the negative energy that was lurking around gathered together in a big bunch of badness. Only no one knows where it came from. Kind of like the aphids. All you can do is control what you can and hope the rest works itself out.

10

Ethan runs up to me in the hall before lunch. He's frantically waving his phone over his head. People stare and smile and part for him in the hall like he's rock star royalty.

"You're not going to believe this," he says.

"What?"

"A major producer heard *Forever*. He wants to sign me for a second album. A *big* second album."

"Oh my god! That's amazing!"

"Zeke said he doesn't even care who backs me. He'll sign whoever I want to record with. He's only interested in me."

"Holy crap."

"The producer just left a message. I'm freaking out."

"Do not freak out. This is what you've been waiting for."

"We knew this was going to happen."

"Totally."

We look at each other for a minute. Then we bust out screaming. We're jumping up and down and laughing and hugging each other. Ethan lifts me up and spins me around right here in the middle of the hall.

Everyone is watching us.

"Keep it moving, people!" the security officer booms. "Let's go! We're on the move!"

No one moves. They want to see what Ethan will do next.

"I have to call him back," he says.

"So call him." We both have lunch next. We could sneak out to Ethan's car if we hurry. The security officer won't notice. He's busy trying to wrangle everyone to class.

"Should I call him back right away?"

"Why not?"

"I don't want to seem too eager."

"But you *are* eager. That's a good thing."

"Won't I look desperate?"

It's cute how Ethan is acting like a girl obsessing over whether to call the boy she likes. I've never seen him this insecure.

"No," I assure him. "You'll look professional. Businesspeople like it when their calls are returned quickly. If you wait, it might come off like you're not serious."

"Good point. But maybe I should talk to Zeke first. I don't want to say the wrong thing."

"So call Zeke."

"Is this really happening?"

"Definitely."

Ethan shakes his head in amazement. "We knew this day would come. You knew it right along with me." There are tears in his eyes. "Thank you for believing in me as much as I believe in myself."

"Of course. You're destined for greatness."

Ethan leans in close. "Get ready for the big time, baby," he whispers in my ear. Then he kisses me.

Everyone is still watching us. Ethan Cross *is* rock star royalty. And from the way they're staring at me, you'd think I was a princess.

11

Forever drops on the first Tuesday of October.
It goes straight to number one.

12

Ethan's album has only been out for a week, but things are already beyond hectic. His website designer had to overhaul the site to accommodate heavy traffic. His mom hired two assistants and a stylist. Zeke brought over a huge bag of fan mail even though most of Ethan's fan mail is emailed to him. Zeke says that Ethan might make history as the last rock star to get this much vintage mail now that most communication is online. Mrs. Cross and Zeke have been discussing bodyguards. Ethan doesn't need 24/7 personal security yet, but he probably will soon. He just signed with that big producer for his second album. Even though he had the chance to record with more experienced musicians, Ethan insisted on recording with his band. Loyalty is important to him. Those guys have been with Ethan from the start. He was disappointed when he couldn't record *Forever* with the band, but now he can make it up to them. Red Bedroom Records was bummed that Ethan's leaving them. But this is what every musician dreams of. There's no way he couldn't open the door for this amazing opportunity when it knocked.

I knock on the open door to Ethan's room. "Hey, you."

He twists around in his desk chair and smiles at me. "Come here, beautiful."

I drop my bags on his bed. Ethan gets up to kiss me. It's been so weird not seeing him at school. This is the third day he's been allowed to stay home to work on publicity stuff. He had four phone interviews this morning—two with radio stations, one with a magazine, and one with a talk show. Then he had a photo shoot in New Haven. Now he's responding to fan comments and updating online.

"I missed you," I say.

"I missed you more."

"How could you even have time to miss me? You're so busy."

"I'm never too busy for you." Ethan puts my hand over his heart. "You're always with me, no matter what I'm doing."

"Your heart's beating fast."

"It's like that when you're around."

Melting. On. The floor.

"What's in the bag?" he asks, noticing the extra shopping bag I dropped on his bed with my book bag.

"Your homework."

"How did you . . . You went to my teachers?"

"No, they left everything for you in the main office. They even let you borrow extra books. Your mom told them I'd bring home whatever you needed."

"Huh." Ethan doesn't look too thrilled about the ton of work he has to make up. "I didn't know she said that."

"Neither did I, until I got called to the main office."

Ethan peers into the big shopping bag. "When am I supposed to have time to do all this?"

"Um, last time I checked you were still in high school."

"That's the problem. I don't have time to do both. You know I'm trying to convince my parents I should be privately tutored."

"Like your dad's really going to let you drop out."

"Mom's working on him. And it wouldn't be dropping out. I'd still have to do the same work. Just not in school." Ethan takes books and papers out of the bag. "So much time is wasted at school anyway. A lot of it is group work. Moving between classes. Teachers trying to get everyone to pay attention. It's not like I need whole periods for gym or lunch. If you took out all that wasted time, the entire school day would probably be like two hours."

Being at school without Ethan would suck. I love having lunch with him. I love knowing he's in the same building as me. The day Gram had her surgery, Ethan walked me to every class so he could hold my hand and tell me everything would be okay. My friends are awesome, but the connection I have with them just isn't the same.

"Did Sydney take my iPod again?" Ethan's searching all over his room. "I've told her a million times to leave my stuff alone."

"Did you check your bag?"

He checks his bag. Then he storms out of his room. I hear him pounding on Sydney's door.

"What?" she yells over her music.

"Did you take my iPod?"

Sydney whips open her door. "I didn't take your stupid iPod, okay?"

"Then where is it?"

"How should I know? Try asking someone who cares."

"You better start caring before I search your room."

"Did I say you could come in?"

"You come in my room all the time."

"No I don't."

"You think I don't know? You and your friends need to keep out."

"Why would we want to go in your gross room? I'm so sick of you making everything about you. Everything is not about you, Ethan!"

"I didn't say it was!"

"What's all that yelling?" Mrs. Cross yells up the stairs. "I'm trying to talk to Ethan's assistants."

"See?" Sydney screeches. "Everything is about you! I am so *sick of it*!" She slams her door.

Ethan comes back to his room. "I still think she took my iPod," he grumbles.

I feel bad for Sydney. I really do. As much as Ethan craves attention from his dad, Sydney must miss the attention she used to get from her mom that's now going to Ethan.

I used to think they were the perfect family. Maybe they were. But not anymore.

13

Ethan Cross and The Invincibles have their first big solo show tonight in New York City. We drove in early with Georgia to explore the city. Drew, Stefan, and Gage are driving the van in with the band's equipment. The show is at Irving Plaza, this historic venue in Gramercy. Gramercy is a small neighborhood with this gorgeous park in the center. But it's a private park. All four gates are locked. Only people who live right along the perimeter of the park have keys. Georgia scoffed at the pretentious keyed park. She did not scoff at the Rice Krispies Treats we scored at this café near the park that were as big as our face. After Rice Krispies Treats nirvana, Ethan wanted to check out some music shops on St. Mark's Place for rare imports. Now we're meeting Zeke for dinner at the Tic Toc Diner.

The first thing you notice about the Tic Toc Diner is that

there are all these cool clocks on the walls. Illuminated 1950s ones. Elaborate neon ones. Ancient ones that clearly stopped working a long time ago and will probably never work again. New York appreciates the retro like that.

Zeke is waving to Ethan from a booth. We go over as Zeke gestures wildly while yelling into the phone.

"No. That won't work. I said *Tuesday*. Wednesday would be too late." Zeke motions for us to slide into the booth. Georgia and I sit across from Zeke. Ethan sits next to him. "That's not my problem. Make it happen." Zeke puts his phone down on the table. The tension in his face converts into a big smile for Georgia. "Georgia, right?" He extends his hand.

Georgia shakes Zeke's hand. "Right." She's kind of marveling at Zeke. He has that power over people. Like everyone should just sit back and let Zeke steer.

"Good to meet you. Any friend of Ethan's is a friend of mine. What can I get everyone to drink?"

After we order, Zeke launches into a discussion with Ethan about his first tour. There's going to be a big announcement about it in a couple of weeks.

"I'm predicting at least five sold-out venues the day tickets go on sale," Zeke says. "Maybe even by noon."

Ethan nods enthusiastically. "That's awesome."

"Don't be surprised when the paparazzi start showing up in your town. Those bastards will hound the crap out of you. But that's what we want."

"Man, I am so ready to be hounded, you don't even know."

"Oh, I know."

"You freaking *know*!" Ethan jams his fist at Zeke. They do exploding pounds.

"We're going to make you a big star," Zeke says. "Be ready."

"I was born ready," Ethan says in a cocky tone. He's half joking. The other half is how he is around Zeke. Sometimes there's this shift in personality people get when they're around certain other people. They sort of become a slightly different person for a while. Most kids I know are like that. But Ethan's only like that around Zeke. He becomes more aggressive or something. Zeke brings out Ethan's hunger for fame in a way he normally doesn't let anyone else see.

There's already a huge line outside when we get to Irving Plaza. The band loaded all the equipment through the side door earlier. We could go in the side door, but Ethan thought it would be fun to go in the front. I watch the fans' expressions as we walk up. A ripple of electricity filters through the crowd as we pass the end of the line.

"Oh my god that's *him*!" one girl shrieks.

Everyone starts screaming. Ethan smiles and waves at the crowd. He loves getting to see his fans in person. The line is roped in. Security guards are keeping everyone behind the ropes. One girl sneaks under the rope and runs up to Ethan. She throws her arms around him. She's squealing so loudly I can't understand what she's saying. Ethan lets her take a quick picture with him. Then we duck inside before everyone else attacks him for pictures.

Ethan has his own dressing room. It's way nicer than the one he shared with the band at The Space. There's a huge cookie plate, bowls of fruit, bagels, and muffins. Drinks are lined up in a clear mini fridge. The polished black stone dressing table is massive. Round, bright lights frame the mirror. A huge bouquet of flowers sits on the dressing table. Ethan goes over to read the card.

"They're from my mom," he says.

Georgia and I are like, "Awww!" We adore how supportive Mrs. Cross is.

"Nice flowers," Gage adds, peering in from the doorway.

"Hey, man," Ethan says. "You ready?"

"Getting there." Gage leans back against the door frame. He stares at the cookie plate.

"Decent spread, huh? Do you guys have like three of everything in your room?"

"Something like that." Gage smirks at me. Ethan doesn't notice, digging through his bag. I understand the resentment behind Gage's smirk. The band's dressing room is nothing like Ethan's. Even though it's for three guys, it's smaller than this one. There's no cookie plate or bowls of fruit or muffins. Just a few stale-looking pastries. I saw their dressing room on the way in, but Ethan obviously hasn't seen it yet.

I try to keep the pity out of my eyes as I look back at Gage. I want him to know I'm sorry he's not getting the same amount of attention as Ethan. But Ethan has worked really hard for this his whole life. He has the kind of natural talent you're either born with or you're not. Although Gage has put a lot of time into songwriting, he's nowhere near the musician Ethan is. Those were the cards Gage was dealt. Whether he continues to be bitter about Ethan's success or starts accepting Ethan's success as a good thing for everyone involved remains to be seen.

Unlike when we had to battle it out with the standing-room-only crowd at The Space, Georgia and I have front row access tonight. The manager escorts us to the front of the crowd. Some girls behind us give us the stink eye. They probably assume we won a contest or something.

"Where's Marisa?" Georgia asks. Marisa agreed to take pictures tonight for Ethan's website. She was stoked that I asked her. Not only because she's a fan of Ethan's, but because she's been looking for more ways to get her photos noticed. This could be a huge opportunity for her if Zeke arranges to sell Marisa's photos online. Maybe she'll even become Ethan's official concert photographer.

"She's on her way." I text Marisa that we're in the front row and to let me know if she has any problems getting up here. Ethan put her on the list.

"So what's happening with Kurt?" I ask. Kurt and Georgia were texting the other day. He didn't ask her out, though.

"A whole lot of nothing. I haven't heard from him."

"At all?"

Georgia shakes her head.

"Do you talk at school?"

"Not really. I saw him in the hall yesterday. He pretended not to see me."

"Maybe he didn't."

"Please. I could feel him pretending not to see me. The

way he was laughing with his friends was so obvious."

"Why don't you ask him out again?"

"Why doesn't he ask *me* out? He knows I'm interested. If he was interested, wouldn't he at least be talking to me?"

"He just texted you."

"Three days ago. Which I can't believe. It feels like three years ago. I'm obsessing over my phone. I can't stop checking it. I'm on permanent Kurt Alert at school. Waiting for something that isn't going to happen is excruciating."

"You don't know it isn't going to happen. He probably just needs time."

"To what? Realize he hates me?"

I put my arm around Georgia. She leans against me. I remember how badly it hurts when you can't stop thinking about a boy who doesn't feel the same way.

Roadies are setting up the band's equipment. Michael Jackson's *Off the Wall* is playing, requested by Ethan. I'm so freaking happy for him. A solo show in New York City is another one of his big dreams he made reality. There will be more New York shows after this one. This show sold out in three hours. The big producer guy who signed Ethan is fast-tracking his second album. Ethan has two more songs to write for it. Then they'll start recording.

I'm about to tell Georgia what Ethan has planned for the lighting effects when a girl behind us goes ballistic.

"This joint is hella dope!" she yells. Then she whoops like such a lunatic her friends have to whoop with her. She leaps up and throws her hands in the air. "Ethan Crooooosss!" she screams. Her friends are chanting. "E-*than*! E-*than*! E-*than*!"

The girl next to me is talking in that loud, authoritative way where you want everyone to hear you because you think you're the only person in the world who possesses such vital information.

"Ethan started taking guitar lessons when he was six," she tells her friend. "That's when he knew he was going to be famous."

"How could he know that young?" her friend asks.

"He just *knew*. He said being megafamous was his fate. But not in an obnoxious way where he just wanted to get rich. He wanted to bring his fans a fresh, new sound that they would love as much as he does. Ethan is all about his fans."

"Totally." Her friend nods emphatically. "He responds to tons of comments. And he always stops to take pictures."

"Like when he was coming in. That girl is *so* lucky."

"I hate her."

"I hate her more."

I wonder how much they would hate me if they knew who I was.

"How awesome is he for coming in the front door like that?" the girl says. "He could have gone around back. It's like he was saying he's one of us. Like he'll never forget where he came from."

"Ethan *Crooooosss*!" the girl behind me screams.

"E-*than*! E-*than*!" her friends chant.

"Damn," Georgia says so only I can hear. "Can you believe this is all for your boyfriend?"

No. I really can't. Everyone here has that giddy-excited-nervous energy you feel before shows. I can hear it in the way their voices are trembling. Where you can't think or talk about anything else while you're waiting for the show to start. Where you can hardly breathe you're so overloaded. Where you have to talk loudly about each and every little thing you've heard about the artist as if you are the authority. As if you're the one who discovered him and you have complete owner-ship over his music. Because you're surrounded by a bunch of wild fans who might think they're as obsessed as you are. But there's no possible way they can be. There's no way any-one else can understand how much his music means to you. How his music is the soundtrack of your life. I can't believe the giddy-excited-nervous energy is for my boyfriend.

"They're playing Michael Jackson because he's one of Ethan's biggest influences," the girl next to me tells her friend.

"I know. So are The Beatles."

"I heard he got signed for his next album, but not with Red Bedroom."

"It's with some really big label."

"Do you know which one?"

"No one's posted anything about it."

"Maybe it was just announced."

They frantically check their devices.

"Sterling!" Marisa lunges up to me, pushing her way through the girls behind us. I can feel the stink eye burning into the back of my head. "Can you believe how crowded it is?"

Marisa and I still hang out sometimes. We're just not as close as we used to be. I'm not really sure why we grew apart. We kind of branched off into our own separate worlds after tenth grade. But we'll always be friends.

"I know!" I yell back. "This is awesome!"

Marisa and Georgia say hey. Then Marisa takes out her professional Nikon camera. Her photography skills are ridiculous. I'm so happy she's documenting Ethan's show. His fans are going to love these photos.

"Have you been backstage?" Marisa asks.

"Yeah. But we can go again after if you want."

"Of course I want. When else am I going to have backstage access?"

"Maybe you'll become a concert photographer."

"Only if you'll publish a book of my photos."

"Done."

When the lights go down and the crowd screams and Ethan comes onstage, I scream louder than anyone. I want to make sure he can hear me.

14

Everyone in Far Hills leaves their doors unlocked. But now that Ethan's getting famous, Mrs. Cross insists on locking the doors. Mr. Cross is still in denial that anyone knows who Ethan is.

I ring Ethan's bell. No one's home. I try the door even though I know it's locked. Then I sit on the front porch steps to wait for him.

Sitting still is not my thing. Yoga isn't helping me to be more present quickly enough. But I keep trying to focus within the confines of my own mat, as my yoga instructor says. I take out the book I'm reading. I've already marked two typos. I'll email the author to let her know about them and any others I find when I finish the book. Letting authors know about typos in their books is something I started doing a few months ago. I was really surprised to hear that no one else told them about the errors. Don't editors read the finished copies of the books they edit? Don't authors read their own books?

I try to focus on my book. But my mind keeps wanting to drift away from the story. I'm wondering where Ethan is. He wasn't at school again today and he said he'd be home by now when we made plans last night. He had a lunch meeting with the big producer guy. Maybe it ran late.

Eleven pages later, Ethan comes up the driveway bouncing a basketball. He looks so cute in his gray hoodie and basketball shorts. He smiles when he sees me.

"Hey, beautiful." He bends down to kiss me. "Sorry I'm late. Miles roped me into a pickup game."

"That's okay."

"How was your day?"

"Gross. I miss you when you're not at school."

"I miss you, too."

I hold my arms out to him.

"I'm all sweaty," he says.

"Do I look like I care?"

He sits on the step next to me. "Better?"

"Much."

"How about . . . when I do this?" Ethan wiggles his fingers near my armpit.

"No!" I shriek. "No tickling!"

"You sure about that? Because I heard there would be tickling."

I scrunch myself into a protective ball. "You heard wrong."

"Maybe I heard it from Steve," Ethan says, throwing

down one of our favorite *Flight of the Conchords* references. Jemaine and Bret diss Steve in their "Hiphopopotamus vs. Rhymenoceros" video.

"Did Steve tell you that, perchance?"

"*Steve.*" Ethan gets up and bounces his basketball. "So did I miss another fascinating day of information we'll never use again or what?"

"Well, I don't know about *fascinating*, but . . ."

"But what?"

"It's school."

"Which you used to hate."

"Which I don't anymore. Now that I know what I want to do with my life." I used to be like Ethan. Hating school. Having no interest in my grades. Doing the minimum to scrape by so I could focus on the things I loved outside of school. Then I decided I wanted to be a publisher. I realized how many doors could open for me if I started taking school seriously. I don't want Ethan to wreck his future the way I almost wrecked mine.

"My future is already decided." Ethan bounces the ball in front of me. "My mom's wearing my dad down on the whole private tutoring thing. He won't have much of an argument when I'm on tour."

Ethan's new record producer struck a deal with Red Bedroom. The new label is putting together a huge tour. In exchange, Red Bedroom agreed that Ethan and his new label will be earning a higher cut of the profits. The producer's argument was that his label had the budget to do a major tour, which will result in way more album sales. Red Bedroom could hardly afford to cover Ethan's travel expenses. Plus Red Bedroom's cut of the tour revenue will be significantly higher with a larger tour. So Ethan's first tour is going to be monumental.

"Couldn't you stay in school until you go on tour?"

"What for?"

"We'd have more time together, for one."

"I'm seeing you as much as I can. Things won't be this crazy forever."

"You'd get an education, for another."

"This is . . ." Ethan gives the ball a few hard bounces. "Everything I've been dreaming about since I was six is finally coming true. You know how hard I've worked for this. I expected you to understand."

"I do understand. I just don't want you to sacrifice your education."

"It's not like I won't be getting a good education. Private tutors are excellent."

That's a tight argument. Maybe wanting Ethan to stay in school is selfish. But our senior year was supposed to be epic. Senior prom. The last high school parties we'll ever go to. Graduation. Now I don't even know if Ethan will be here for any of those things.

We must look like typical teens to anyone watching us. Girlfriend sitting on the porch. Boyfriend bouncing a basketball. The sun dipping behind the trees, throwing orange streaks of light across them. Just your average American high school sweethearts on a fall afternoon.

It's amazing how what we assume about other people can be so different from the truth.

15

Ethan did two more TV appearances this week. One was for *Good Morning America*, which has about five million viewers a day. The other was for an afternoon talk show with about six million viewers. So now eleven million people have seen Ethan. More than eleven million, counting his fans.

That might be why a photographer is snapping pictures of us from across the street.

A stranger danger red flag went up when I first noticed this guy lurking. I saw him when Ethan and I came out of my place. He had been leaning against the fence of the house across from my building. When he saw us leaving, he whipped out his camera. His camera has a superlong lens. Good thing the living room blinds were closed.

We walk to Ethan's car. The photographer follows us, wildly snapping pictures. He even scoots in front of me on the sidewalk when we get to Ethan's car.

"Hey, buddy," Ethan says in a friendly way. "Can I open the door for my girlfriend here?"

"Sure thing, Ethan," the guy says. He's still snapping pictures.

We get in the car. Ethan pulls away from the curb. I watch the guy run to his car across the street.

"You think he's going to follow us?" Ethan says.

The guy's car zooms up right in back of Ethan's. I'm surprised he didn't hit us.

"Hmmm," I say. "It's hard to tell."

We get to the Notch and park in the lot. As soon as we get out, the camera's up on us again. Ethan holds my hand as we walk to the entrance. We're both smiling. Ethan's smiling because he's a rock star. I'm smiling because I'm starting to really like being a rock star's girlfriend.

Not that it's always good times. When Mom and I were grocery shopping last weekend, she noticed this lady following us around.

"Isn't that the same woman who was trying those crostini samples with us?" she whispered to me. Stalker Lady was pushing her cart a few steps behind us.

I turned halfway around, pretending to examine the canned soups.

"Yeah," I said. "Why?"

"She's been following us for three aisles."

"Are you sure?"

"Yes." Mom turned to face Stalker Lady. "May we help you?"

Stalker Lady was startled. She had no idea she'd been made.

"I'm so sorry," she stuttered. "I was . . . I saw Sterling when you came in. My daughter is a big fan of Ethan's." She looked at me. "Would you—I'm sorry to bother you like this, but I promised my daughter I'd ask for an autograph if I saw you."

"Oh. Um . . ." I wasn't sure if she wanted my autograph or for me to get one from Ethan.

"This is highly inappropriate," Mom interjected. "Please don't approach my daughter again." She whisked us over to the next aisle, gripping our cart hard. Mom was clearly rattled. Obsessive behavior is one reason she's not into pop culture. She just doesn't understand how someone could whip themselves into such a frenzy that things like common sense and courtesy go out the window.

The kind of attention I get in other stores and restaurants is more fun. A barista at the coffeehouse gives me free pumpkin muffins. And my mom and I always get window tables when we go out to eat. Perks like those are pretty sweet.

"Ethan!" someone yells by the Notch entrance. "Over here!"

A small group of paparazzi are gathered to the left of the front doors. They're snapping pictures of us.

"What do we do?" I ask Ethan when we get close to them.

"We keep doing our thing. They're not allowed to follow us in."

Here's one thing I quickly realized: we don't know where these paparazzi are from. These pictures could show up anywhere. If they take one bad picture and post it, it could haunt us forever.

"Want to stand here for a minute so they can get some good shots?" Ethan asks.

"Okay."

"Looking good, Sterling!" one of the paps yells.

Holy crap.

They know my name.

They know who I *am*.

This fame thing isn't just about Ethan anymore. When I'm out with him, I'm representing him in a way no one else can. Before I was fighting change. I was sad about not seeing Ethan at school. Worried about what leaving school would do to his future. Upset that I didn't get to see him as much as I used to. But instead of fighting change, I need to embrace change. That's what I've been learning in yoga. Change is a natural part of life. It's the only way we can grow and evolve and become stronger. Change is how we create the life we want to be living. My yoga instructor has a favorite quote about how the stiff will be broken but the flexible will prevail. I want to be a supple willow in the breeze. Not a sharp branch that snaps at the first sign of trouble.

I stand up straighter. I remember to engage my core like we do in yoga. My face hurts from smiling.

The paparazzi stay outside the Notch when we go in. A bunch of people who were watching them take pictures come in with us. You can tell they know who Ethan is. They're staring at us as we head to Shake Shack. It's weird how we can feel their cloud of nervous excitement pressing into us, but we kind of have to pretend we don't notice them.

Ethan is stoked by the attention. He's doing his best not to show it, though. He doesn't want to come off as obnoxious.

We go into Shake Shack. A few people who were following behind us almost trip over one another. Almost everyone in Shake Shack looks up. There's that electric vibe again. The one that sparks whenever Ethan walks into a room.

This is only the beginning. Ethan is just starting to break out. If things are this crazy now, what will it be like when he's insanely famous?

16

A nurse stayed with Gram for a week after she came back from the hospital. Gram wasn't doing too well at first. But she's feeling way better now. She's into her usual activities of bingo, baking, and cards with her girls. She even went back to her aqua aerobics class last week. Gram's doctor says she's kicking some serious angioplasty butt.

I go around to the back of Gram's house. She's probably in the kitchen baking cookies from Betty Crocker's *Cookie Book*. She knows I love the Ultimate Spritz cookies.

Gram sees me through her kitchen window above the sink. She waves me in.

"Ya-*hum*!" I kiss her hello on the cheek. "It smells so good in here!"

"There's nothing like the smell of fresh-baked cookies," Gram agrees.

"Unless it's fresh-baked brownies."

"Oooh, I just found a new recipe for triple chocolate peanut butter brownies with fudge frosting. I'll have to try those next."

"Or I could just move in and you could bake them for me every day."

"I think you do a pretty good job of that yourself."

"The baking master taught me everything I know."

"Well. I don't know about that."

"Have you seen these cookies? They look even better than the photo." The art of the spritz cookie is a delicate dance. You have to know your way around a cookie press. You have to be precise when shaping the cookies. When you decorate spritz cookies after they bake, you have to use a drop of corn syrup to attach the sprinkles. If you're not precise, the cookies could easily be ruined. It's an extensive process that requires hours of dedication.

Gram adds more sprinkles to her star-shaped cookies.

"How are you feeling?" I ask.

"Like a new woman. Being back in the swing of things is invigorating. I even won at bingo!"

"Yay! How much?"

"Thirty-nine dollars. Not a bad haul."

"Not bad at all."

I watch Gram putting the final decorations on the cookies. I take deep breaths, inhaling the warm sugary scent of my childhood. We spent so many afternoons together like this when I came over after school. Mom didn't want me home alone before I was in high school. I would get off the bus and come over to Gram's. She always had a special snack waiting for me, usually something baked fresh. Gram always wanted to know what was going on with me. She wasn't asking in that typical polite way. She really wanted us to share our lives. This kitchen tells our history. So many memories I cherish the most were made between these walls.

After the cookies are decorated, Gram gets a magazine from the breakfast table. "Look what I found." The magazine she's holding up isn't just any magazine. It's a major celeb gossip magazine. With a picture of me and Ethan from the paparazzi swarm last week.

"How did you know about this?" I ask.

"I told you, I'm back in the swing of things, my dear. I know everything."

Gram heard about the paparazzi along with everyone else in town. But I didn't tell her which magazine the picture showed up in. Of course I was stoked when I saw it. I just don't like the way I look. A few other pictures showed up online from the same day. What I'm wearing is cute, but it lacks that cool/comfortable/collected ensemble look every other girl on the couples pages is rocking. They seem to pull off that look effortlessly. As if everything in their closet perfectly fits together. Meanwhile, I tried on fifteen different outfits before Ethan's last show and still ended up hating what I was wearing. Those other girls in the magazine are all celebs. They can afford the most expensive clothes and accessories. I'll have to find my own way to step it up.

Gram flips the magazine open to where it's marked with a Post-it. "Nice picture of you and Ethan." She traces her finger over the picture.

"I don't really like it. That's why I didn't show it to you."

"Why don't you like it? You two look adorable!"

I look at the pages for the millionth time. It's not like me to obsess over styles or hair or whatever. But those other girls are so beautiful. They're so glamorous while I'm . . . sticking out like I don't belong.

"The other girls are so much prettier than me," I say.

"You hush with that nonsense. No one is prettier than you."

"Are we looking at the same pictures?"

"You are a beautiful, intelligent, radiant girl. That's who I'm looking at."

Part of me desperately wants to tell Gram about my other insecurities. About the fear of losing Ethan when he achieves insane fame. It came crashing in after those paparazzi followed us to the Notch and has been growing ever since. But I don't want to worry Gram with the anxiety part of being Ethan's girlfriend. She loves that he's becoming more successful every day. She loves that I'm part of all the excitement.

I'm beyond happy for Ethan. I should focus on the amazing parts of this ride instead of worrying about what I can't control. Because when else will something this spectacular happen?

17

Today is one of those rare days when Ethan is actually at school. I never realized how much I used to take the simple things for granted. Like Ethan driving me to school or sitting with me at lunch or kissing me in the hall. Having Ethan next to me here at our lunch table, his arm around me while he laughs at a story Miles is telling, I can't imagine ever taking those things for granted again.

Miles and Ethan have been friends since they were little. They built a fort in the woods together in fifth grade. Ethan brought me there when we started going out. The fort was really worn down. It had a lot of missing boards and a big piece of the ceiling was gone. But the history of their friendship was almost tangible, built into the fort's construction.

Now that Miles and Ethan are seniors, the attention they gave the fort has been replaced by a strong focus on girls. Miles and his girlfriend, Reyna, sit with us at lunch. We double-dated with them a lot, back before Ethan started blowing up. And we hung out with our other friends a few times a week. Ethan doesn't see his friends that much anymore. The only time I see Miles and Reyna these days is at lunch. They're more his friends than mine.

Everyone at the table is freaking out over Ethan's first tour. It was announced this morning. Ethan said keeping the tour a secret until it was officially announced was the hardest thing he'd ever had to do. He told me about the tour, but I had to lock it in the vault.

"So when does your tour start?" Reyna asks.

"January. It's a three-month run."

"How many shows is it?" Miles asks.

"Forty-six."

"Damn, son! All famous and shit."

"I wish."

"Seriously?" Reyna says. "Forty-six shows is amazing."

"Congrats, man." Miles and Ethan pound fists.

"Everything's happening so fast," I say. "It's unreal." I remember hearing "Night on Fire" on the radio for the first time. That was last month. Now Ethan has three singles out. They're all getting major radio play. You can't have Z100 on for more than an hour without hearing one of his songs.

"That shirt is fierce," Reyna tells Ethan. "Where did you get it?"

"It was a gift from the designer. She sent it to Zeke for me." Ethan's wearing a Pacey Witter–type bowling shirt made of distressed silk. It's black with two white stripes down the front. He looks really good in it.

"Sweet."

"Ethan gets major swag," I say. "Everyone's sending him their designs."

"Because they're fans, or . . . ?" Reyna asks.

"They're hoping pictures or videos of me wearing their stuff will show up. Apparently they do this a lot with celebs. Not sure why they're bothering with me. But I'm not complaining."

"I love those chains," a girl I don't know at the end of the table says. "Are they platinum?"

Ethan nods.

"Can a best friend get a hookup?" Miles wants to know.

"Borrow whatever you want. The only stuff I have to send back is what's out on loan for appearances."

"Your life is amazing." Reyna sighs. "I want to be you when I grow up."

Ethan laughs. "You want to train six days a week and rehearse four hours a day? Be my guest."

"Ugh, no, that's too hard."

"My trainer doesn't even let me eat what Sterling makes anymore."

"He does if it's on the list," I say.

"What list?" Miles asks.

"My trainer gave me a list of what I'm allowed to eat. If it's not on the list, I can't eat it."

I love cooking for Ethan. But he's so determined to stick to the list that he hardly lets me anymore. Even when I make something that's on the list, he only eats half the amount he used to. And we can't have our fun dinners and snacks at Shake Shack after school anymore because his schedule is so crazy.

"That sucks." Miles takes a huge bite of chocolate cake. "I bet cake's not on the list, huh?"

"Not so much. My trainer would kill me."

I know Ethan's training is super important. He has a grueling tour coming up. Zeke decided Ethan should take things to the next level with this big tour. There will be choreography for some songs. There will even be backup dancers. Ethan is nervous, even though he's an amazing dancer. He wants to make sure the choreo is perfect. Staying in maximum shape is crucial. But if I hear him say "my trainer" one more time, I'm going to lose it.

"You guys looked so cute on *GMA*," Reyna says.

It was a total surprise when *Good Morning America* flashed a picture of me and Ethan. They asked him about his girlfriend and he told them my name and there we were. Filling up the TV screens of millions of people.

Ethan leans up against me to whisper in my ear. "You looked beautiful. Just like today and every other day I've known you."

Melting. Into. My chair.

The girl at the end of the table keeps sneaking glances at

me. I recognize the look in her eyes. I've been seeing it more and more. The longing. The jealousy. Wishing she could switch places with me. I don't think I'll ever get used to being on this side of that look.

But I'm happy to be here.

18

The first week of November means one thing in my town. It's Harvest time.

The Harvest Festival is an annual event on the river. We just call it the Harvest. It's kind of a festival with booths selling treats and clothes and knickknacks, mostly made by people who live here. There are games and contests. Everyone comes out for it.

I've been baking for the Harvest since seventh grade. Gram ran our booth back then. Now I run it. Gram says I've outdone myself this year. That's because I suddenly have all this free time. The time I'd normally be spending with Ethan is like this gaping void in my life. I've been filling the void by baking enough cookies, cupcakes, brownies, and pies to feed a small country. According to Gram, my baking is legendary. She insists that my heart cookies are famous. She likes to exaggerate. But my favorite coffeehouse does stock them when I have enough time to make a few large batches.

My heart cookies are abundant today. They're wrapped in opalescent cellophane and tied with different colored ribbons. It's kind of my signature style. I used to hang the cookies from skinny tree branches I assembled over the table. This year I wanted to do something different with their presentation. The cookies are gathered in cute heart baskets I bought from another local entrepreneur.

Georgia is working the booth with me. After we arrange all the treats in groups, we sit on rickety folding chairs to await customers seeking sugar. We don't have to wait long before a group of girls from school comes over.

"Hey, Sterling!" Kelsey goes. As if we're friends.

"Hey."

"You know Markita and Ravyne, right?"

I give them a weak smile. These girls have a seriously twisted view of the world. They think that just because they're on cheer squad that gives them the right to torment anyone who dares to be unpopular. I once saw Kelsey put a Godiva truffle on Lynn Sweitzer's chair in class before she sat down. That poor girl sat right on the chocolate. Kelsey and Markita snickered all through class. Lynn had no idea what was happening. I had to pass her a note to break the news. I couldn't stand the thought of Lynn getting up when class was over and walking out with a rude chocolate smear on her butt. So yeah. These girls are not my friends.

Not that it's stopping them from acting like they are.

"Are you *so* excited for Ethan's tour?" Kelsey gushes.

"Of course," I say.

"Why isn't he doing a show in Connecticut?" Markita asks.

"Yeah," Ravyne chimes in. "I thought he'd be hitting Hartford. Since he's from here and all."

"Ethan doesn't decide where he goes," I explain. "The production company and his manager arrange the schedules."

"Oh." Kelsey sniffs. "Well, I guess I'll go see him at Madison Square Garden. It's so hot he's playing there."

"*So* hot," Ravyne confirms.

"Wouldn't it be awesome if we could get comped tickets?" Kelsey fishes. "Let's see . . . who do we know who knows Ethan?"

These girls have never talked to me before. Now they're asking for free tickets to a show that will probably be sold out?

"Sorry, I can't get you in," I say. "I have no control over that."

"Really? You can't pull some strings?"

"Why should she?" Georgia, who has been watching in silent disgust this whole time, can't stay quiet anymore. "You're not even friends."

"Whatever, freak. Don't you mow my lawn or something?"

Markita and Ravyne laugh nastily. Georgia has an internship with Marisa's Aunt Katie, who has her own landscaping company. She's not interested in mowing lawns. She's learning how to transform any yard into a beautiful landscape. Which is a lot more than these beeyotches will ever do.

"Did you want to buy something?" I ask. "There's a line."

"We don't eat desserts," Kelsey informs me. "We're on cheer?"

"Have fun with that," Georgia says.

The girls huff off.

"Where does Kelsey get off thinking she can manipulate everyone?" Georgia seethes.

"Profound ignorance will do that to you."

Mrs. Kennedy, who was standing behind the girls all oblivious to their snark, swoops up to the table. She's one of my best customers.

"Sterling! I can't tell you how happy I am to see you."

"Hi, Mrs. Kennedy. This is my friend Georgia."

"Nice to meet you, Georgia. Do you know how delicious Sterling's baking is?"

"Totally. She's my sugar mama."

"Everything looks so good!" Mrs. Kennedy has been buying from me since my first year at the Harvest. She bought from Gram for years before that. Mrs. Kennedy is probably tired of doing her own baking. She has four kids.

"You should run a catering business, Sterling," Mrs. Cherski tells me as she passes by my table on the way to her own. She knits the most adorable hats.

"I've been telling her that for years!" Mrs. Kennedy says. Which is true. She tells me every year. Feedback like theirs makes me think about how I could do more with my life. Ethan's success is pushing me to be more ambitious. I had this idea for a cooking video series. It would be a fun way to share recipes and tips. Maybe I could gear the videos toward cooking advice for teens and college students.

"We can only hope," Mrs. Cherski says. "I'll stop by later, hon. Did you make some of those chocolate peanut butter fudge brownies your grandmother was telling me about?"

"Right here." I point to the tray.

"Those look incredible," Mrs. Kennedy says. "I'll take half a dozen. You know what? Let's do a dozen. And I'll take two cherry pies, two blueberry pies, and a dozen heart cookies. Oh, and a vanilla cupcake. That one's for me."

Georgia raises her eyebrows at me. She starts lifting brownies out of the pan with a spatula to place in a pink pastry box.

"Wow," I say. "Thank you." Mrs. Kennedy just ordered twice what she normally does.

"Thank *you* for the delicious treats. College is so expensive these days. I'm happy to contribute."

Georgia and I put the order together. We pack the pink pastry boxes into a shopping bag.

"Thanks again," I say.

"I hate to ask you this, but . . ." Mrs. Kennedy pulls a folded piece of paper out of her bag. "Could you give this to Ethan from my daughter? She's eleven now, if you can believe that. She's such a big fan."

I'm shocked that Mrs. Kennedy is slipping me a note for Ethan. She's a classic soccer mom. I thought she would be one person I could count on not to get crazy-stalker-fangirl on me.

"Sure." I take the note from her.

"Oh, you're the best." Mrs. Kennedy picks up the shopping bag. "Have a good day, girls!"

"Bye," Georgia says.

We watch the activity at the other tables for a minute. Then Georgia says, "Can I talk to you about something?"

"Of course. Why are you even asking?"

"It's kind of . . . complicated."

"What?"

"Remember when—"

"Hey!" A group of four middle-school girls comes rushing up to the table. "You're Sterling, right?"

"Yeah."

"OMG it's *her*," one girl says. "Can we get a picture?"

"Of what?"

"We want pictures with you!" she giggles. "Is that okay?"

"Oh. Um. I guess." Why would anyone want a picture with me?

She comes around the table and bends down next to me. Her friends snap photos.

"Now me!" another girl shouts. They all take turns getting pictures.

After they run off in a squealing herd of giggles, I ask Georgia what she was going to say before.

"Can't talk now," she says. "We have customers."

The line is so long at one point that I don't even notice Miles and Reyna until they're next. Georgia takes the next person in line while I talk to them.

"You guys didn't have to wait in line," I tell them. "You could have just come around."

"Cutting in line is beneath us," Reyna says.

"Yeah," Miles says. "We prefer to wait with the common folk."

"I heard your chocolate peanut butter fudge brownies are ridonculous," Reyna informs me.

"Want one?"

"More like ten," Miles says. "But we'll manage with one if that's all you've got."

"Actually . . ." I check the chocolate peanut butter fudge brownie pan. "There are exactly two left."

"It's fate," Reyna says.

I pack them up.

"So I haven't seen Ethan for a couple weeks," Miles says. "How's he doing?"

"He's awesome."

"Gearing up for the tour?"

"Totally."

Miles shifts awkwardly, scuffing his shoe on the grass.

"I hardly see him anymore, either," I reassure him.

"You're not missing out on much. That dude's the biggest dork I know."

Reyna swats his arm with the brownie bag. "Be nice."

"If you talk to Ethan, tell him we said hey."

"Will do."

The next two hours are nonstop busy. The whole town is acting like obsessed superfans. Even dads and grandmas who have obviously never heard Ethan's music. Ethan being from here is enough for them to worship him. In a small town like Far Hills, having someone famous living here is probably the most exciting thing that will ever happen.

My cookies sell out in record time. Then I notice we're out of everything else.

"Guess we're done," Georgia says. She springs up from her chair, almost tipping it over. She starts quickly packing up pans and spatulas.

"I can't believe it. I've never sold out that fast."

"You're rock star royalty now. Ethan isn't the only one people are obsessing over."

"As if that makes sense. Who am I?"

"The girl who just sold out in record time. Doesn't hurt to have a famous boyfriend, huh?"

Maybe it's just me, but I'm picking up on some prickly energy from Georgia. She can't get out of here fast enough.

"Are you okay?" I ask.

"Who, me? Why wouldn't I be?"

"I don't know. . . ."

"Don't worry about it."

"Georgia. If something's wrong—"

"Nothing's wrong. Can you please drop it?"

"Not if something's wrong. I want to know what it is. I want to help you."

But Georgia doesn't say anything. She just keeps stacking pans.

We pack up the rest of my stuff in silence.

19

[6,837,328 FOLLOWERS]

There's nothing better than Cosmic Bowling when you're in the mood for dorktastic fabulousness. Their lanes light up. They have glow-in-the-dark bowling balls. Their shoes have white stripes that gleam in the black light. I'm wearing the MY BOYFRIEND IS A ROCK STAR tee Ethan gave me. The white glitter around the star looks fierce.

My shirt doesn't lie. Ethan's tour already has five sold-out venues. Just as Zeke predicted. Including Madison Square Garden. Which holds about fifteen thousand people.

Ethan is blowing up faster than even he imagined.

He goes up to roll. The fog machine is on. I watch Ethan take his turn in the fog, picturing what he'll look like in the fog onstage. I heard they're doing fog in the middle of "Now and Forever." He's going to look amazing. The Forever Tour is going to be epic.

I'm in a daze thinking about the tour when Ethan sits back down next to me after his turn.

"Are you stoked?" he asks.

"For what?"

"The tour."

"I was just thinking about that." Ethan wants me to come on part of the tour with him. Before we left for bowling, my mom said I could miss a few days of school for it. She understands about taking opportunities that come around once in a lifetime. Of course I can't wait to go.

I think I see Georgia coming toward our lane. But that happy burst of adrenaline fades when I realize it's not her. I called Georgia before I left for bowling to invite her along. I asked her to call me back even if she didn't want to come. She never called. Knowing something's wrong that she doesn't want to talk about has been making me nervous ever since the Harvest.

"Um." A girl is lurking by our chairs. "Excuse me. Ethan?" She's clutching a camera.

"Hey." He smiles at her warmly.

"I'm a huge fan. You're my favorite artist."

"Thank you."

"Could I get a picture with you?"

"Let's do it." Ethan stands up to pose next to her. The girl seems to be by herself.

"Could you . . . ?" She holds the camera out to me.

"Sure." I take a picture of my boyfriend with his fan. One

fan among millions. I wonder how many more pictures like this I will take.

"Thank you *so* much," she gushes.

"You're welcome."

This would normally be where the girl leaves to squee over her picture and Ethan and I get back to bowling. Except she's not leaving.

We look at her expectantly.

"So . . . you're really bowling?" she asks.

"I love bowling," Ethan says.

"Same! That's why I'm here. Duh, obviously. My family's over there."

"Cool. Well . . . it was awesome meeting you. Take care."

"You take care, too!" the girl warbles. Then she bolts.

"Awkward," I say.

"She was sweet. At least one girl here is impressed with me."

"When have I not been impressed with you?"

"I don't see you asking for pictures."

"Ethan Cross!" I fling my arms around him. "I love you! I'm your biggest fan! Could you *pleeeeease* take a picture with me?"

"Absolutely." Ethan holds his phone out in front of us. We press our faces together, my cheek touching his.

We smile for the camera.

20

Georgia's trying my yoga class. She's been saying she wants to try it. I've had this queasy feeling in the pit of my stomach about us ever since the Harvest last week. We haven't really talked since then. It's not like Georgia to ignore my calls. When she finally called me back, she just said she's been busy. We're obviously in need of some quality vinyasa time.

This part near the end of class, when we sit cross-legged with the backs of our hands resting on our knees, eyes closed, and breathing deeply in lotus, is my favorite part. Practicing silence is a lot harder than it sounds. I always say I'm going to take time to sit like this every day for five minutes. Just five minutes a day to focus on breathing. Five minutes to be completely calm. To be completely in the Now. But it never works out. I'm always too busy or too preoccupied. This is the only time I truly experience being one with myself.

The class apparently worked for Georgia. She's acting like her old self on our way to the gym's juice bar.

"I'm sorry we didn't get to talk at the Harvest," I say.

"No, *I'm* sorry I acted like such a spaz. There was a lot going on. It's not your fault everyone was bothering you about Ethan."

"They weren't bothering me. It's incredible that everyone's into him."

"You handled it like a pro."

I smile at Georgia. It's a huge relief to get back to our normal energy.

A glaring typo on a sign at the juice bar wipes the smile off my face.

"Excuse me," I say to the cashier. "Your sign has a typo."

"Where?"

I point to the *its* in TRY OUR PINEAPPLE TANGERINE SMOOTHIE. ITS YUMMO! "That should actually be 'it's' with an apostrophe. As in 'it is.'"

The cashier gives me a blank look.

"You can use my marker to correct the sign if you want."

More blank look. I don't know if it's because she doesn't understand what I'm saying or because she doesn't care. "We're not allowed to write on the signs."

"Even when they're wrong?"

"My manager said not to write on them."

"Maybe you could ask your manager to fix the sign?"

"I'll leave him a message."

"Thanks." She probably won't tell him anything. Very few people are sympathetic to my mission. People who work in stores where I've pointed out errors on signs think I'm filing a complaint against them or something. They just don't get that I'm trying to help.

Georgia and I take our juices to the side bar. The bar runs against a glass wall that looks out on the cardio floor. There are always hot guys on the machines. We immediately start scoping out guys for her.

"What about him?" I ask.

"Who?"

"Red shirt on the treadmill."

"He's okay."

"You don't think he's cute?"

"I could do better." Georgia smiles into her Rejuvenate.

"Oh? Like with who?"

"Kurt."

"Wait. Kurt? As in Kurt who sent you some lame texts and then went MIA?"

"Things change."

"He asked you out?"

Georgia nods.

"That's awesome! When?"

"Last night. It was amazing. I didn't think he'd ever talk to me again."

"Why did it take him so long?"

"I don't know. It's weird. This whole time I thought he was avoiding me because he didn't like me. He even ignored me when I went up to him last week. I saw him at his locker and said hi and he hardly even looked at me. That's what I was trying to tell you at the Harvest. But it's all good now. He called me last night and we talked for over an hour."

"But then why did he ignore you last week?"

"He said he was nervous. Seeing me in the hall suddenly caught him off guard or something."

"When are you going out?"

"Next Saturday."

"Where?"

"He said he wants to surprise me."

"Love that."

"Right?!"

"What are you going to wear?"

"I'm not sure. How do I know what to wear if I don't know where we're going?"

"Just do jeans and a dressy top. You'll be ready for anything." I'd love to discuss her date ensemble in detail. But Georgia isn't really into clothes. Her style is more tomboy than girly.

"So guess what?" I say.

"Martha Stewart invited you to her next dinner party."

"My mom's letting me go on part of Ethan's tour." I smile into my Replenish.

"Seriously?"

I nod.

"But where will you stay?"

"At Ethan's hotels. The only reason my mom's okay with it is that I'll have my own room. She doesn't need to know that my room and Ethan's room will technically be connecting rooms in a suite. We can go in and out of each other's rooms without his bodyguards or anyone knowing."

"I thought he didn't have bodyguards yet."

"He has to get them for the tour."

"That's intense. Who would have imagined Ethan Cross would have bodyguards one day?"

"Ethan. He imagined all of this a long time ago."

"Truth."

"I seriously cannot wait for the tour."

"It sounds amazing," Georgia says. Only she says it with less enthusiasm than I was hoping for. I've been dying to tell her about the tour so we could both freak out. Buzzing with anticipation over her freaking out was making me even more excited for the tour.

Why isn't she freaking out?

Georgia pulls the latest *Seventeen* magazine out of her bag. She flips to a dog-eared page. "Let's take this relationship quiz."

"Bring it." Ever since Ethan and I started going out, I've loved taking these quizzes. They always say that Ethan and I are perfect together. Not that I need a quiz to tell me that. We love being together. We make each other happy. And we have tons in common. That's why we've been together for over eight months.

Georgia reads the first question. "On a typical Saturday night, you and your BF: A. Do dinner and a movie. B. Stay in and snuggle on the couch. C. Avoid making plans, opting for spontaneity. D. Attend a book reading."

"C," I tell her. "We're all about being spontaneous."

"In Far Hills?"

"You'd be surprised."

"I'm going with A. Kurt's probably planning something classic for our first date."

"I can't wait to find out where he takes you."

"Dude. I'm getting nervous just thinking about it. Next question. The scenario that best describes your ideal relationship is: A. Going out with mutual friends every week. B. Lots of kissing and romantic gestures. C. Sharing exciting new adventures. D. Geeking out over activities you both enjoy."

"Hmm. Can I pick A, B, and C?"

"Nope. Only one."

"This is too hard. They should ask which scenario best describes the relationship you don't want."

"Really. Like, which scenario best describes the worst relationship ever? A. Long-distance. B. All of the above."

"You were right to break up with Andy."

"I know. I'm feeling much better about it now that I'm going out with Kurt."

"Now that Kurt's about to be your boyfriend."

"Don't jinx it," Georgia warns.

"I know what I don't want." I point to a profusely sweating, overweight, middle-aged guy huffing on an elliptical. More like dying on an elliptical. "Please tell me that's not my husband in twenty years."

"Ethan would never get sloppy. He's too gorgeous."

"Maybe that guy was gorgeous in his teens. We don't know."

"But we know what we want. And we know what we don't want. So the chances of ending up with the right person have already increased dramatically."

Georgia's right. Finding the best relationship is all about visualizing what you want and then refusing to settle for anything less. That's why I'm so happy with Ethan. We have the ideal relationship. Minus spending all this time apart. But like Ethan said, things will get back to normal. Probably not soon. But eventually.

21

I remember the first time Ethan talked to me. It was March 21. I remember how blue the sky was that day. Almost impossibly blue, like I was watching a movie where the color of the sky had been enhanced. My first thought when I woke up that morning and saw the sky was *This will be a good day.*

Ethan came up to me at my locker before algebra. I was trying not to freak out. Ethan Cross was the cutest boy in our class. In the whole school, even. I'm not the kind of girl the cutest boy talks to.

"Hey," he said. Like it was the most natural thing in the world.

"Hey."

"I like your purple streak."

"You do?" I touched my hair self-consciously. I couldn't tell if he was teasing.

"I do. It's badass."

"Thanks."

"What shade of purple is that?"

"Purple Haze."

"Nice. Are you into live music?"

"Who isn't?"

"Do you want to go to a show with me this Saturday? Overlord is playing at The Space in New Haven. Have you been there?"

"No. I mean, yes, I want to go, but I haven't been there."

"You'll love it. Pick you up at seven?"

"Okay."

I was in a purple haze for the rest of the day. Going through the motions. Not hearing one word my teachers said. Going home and spacing out on my bed and getting halfway through cooking dinner before I remembered that Mom wanted to order in. I couldn't believe I was going out with Ethan Cross.

We've been inseparable ever since.

Or . . . we were. Before Ethan blew up. I hardly see him anymore. Ethan's mom finally convinced his dad that private tutoring was the only viable option. He's been officially pulled out of school. Ethan has tutors for each subject who meet up with him at home or in the studio where he's rehearsing for his tour. They'll travel with him when his tour starts.

Actually, an entire entourage will travel with him. I had no idea how many people were involved in a tour. Not only are there the essential players—Ethan, Gage, Drew, Stefan, Zeke, his choreographer, his vocal coach, his nutritionist, his stylist, his bodyguards—but the whole crew is like fifty people. There are experts who take care of the instruments. There are roadies in charge of setting up and breaking down the stage. There's a lighting director and a makeup artist and a costume designer. Plus a lot of these people have assistants.

My boyfriend rolls deep.

Ethan explained all of this to me over the phone. He's been spending most of his time rehearsing and doing marketing stuff. And he's on a major radio/TV promotion spree. I haven't seen him in eight days.

"I miss you," Ethan tells me on the phone.

"When can I see you?"

"Tomorrow. Wait, let me check . . . crap. I'm not going to be here."

"Where are you going?"

"New York. I'm booked for the *Today* show."

"Oh, yeah. I can't believe I forgot. That's huge."

"We have to get there crazy early. Then these big record execs are taking me to lunch. Then I have an interview with *Details* that afternoon."

"Big day."

"I'm already exhausted."

"What time will you be home?"

"Probably not until midnight. Zeke wants me to have dinner with a few of his people."

"So . . . when can I see you?"

"What are you doing right now?"

It's nine thirty on a school night. I was doing my homework when Ethan called.

"Nothing," I say.

"Is your mom home?"

"No."

"Can I come over?"

The thought of seeing Ethan after all this time makes my heart race. Feeling his lips on mine. His hands all over me. Pressing up against each other in bed. I can't wait to touch him again. I know I should finish my homework. But it's been forever.

"How fast can you get here?" I say.

22

Ethan and I are going to an über fancy benefit tonight in New York City. It's at the Waldorf Astoria. I've wanted to go to that hotel ever since I saw *Serendipity*. The scene where Sara is waiting by the elevators hoping that Jonathan pressed the same floor she did was legendary. The benefit is one of those twenty-thousand-dollars-a-plate functions guaranteed to be packed with celebs. I can't believe I'll get to see so many of my favorite actors in one place. We're taking a stretch limo there and back. It will be my first time in a limo.

Tonight is going to be fantastic.

I started getting ready early this afternoon in an effort to look perfect. Or as perfect as I can hope to look. It took me over two hours to get ready. Half an hour of which was spent creating smoky eyes. My dress is floaty, my heels are four inches, and my clutch is beaded. Hopefully, I look presentable.

"You look like a doll," Ethan says when he sees me. He rang my bell even though I told him I could meet him out at the limo. He wanted to escort me down the walkway. He's such a gentleman.

"Thanks," I say, blushing. "I'll get my coat."

"Make sure it's a warm one. It's freezing."

The only coat I have that's dressy enough for an event like this has no insulation. But we're just going from the limo to the hotel and back. I take the long, thin, black coat out of the hall closet. Ethan comes up behind me, taking the coat from me.

"Let me help you," he says.

He holds the coat open. I slide my right arm in, feeling Ethan's breath on my neck. Ever since he came over last week after we hadn't seen each other for eight days, there's been this electricity between us. I mean, there's always been electricity between us. But now it's supercharged.

I slide my left arm in. Ethan hugs me from behind.

"How are you so beautiful?" he says.

Melting. In. The foyer.

We go out to the white stretch limo. No paparazzi are around. I guess they're all waiting for us at the red carpet. The chauffeur gets out and comes around to our side. He holds the door open for us.

"Thank you," I say. A chauffeur holding a door open for me is so fancy I'm almost embarrassed. Ethan climbs in. The door closes behind him.

I can't believe how much room there is back here. There are condos in my building smaller than the back of this limo. The space is tricked out with a mini fridge, two video screens, a tray of champagne glasses with an ice bucket, tons of snacks, and throw pillows. We could live here for days.

The partition between us and the chauffeur is up. We could do anything back here. He would never know.

"This joint has a sick sound system," Ethan says. He turns on Z100. Then he reaches for two champagne glasses. "May I interest you in an adult beverage, mademoiselle?"

"They have adult beverages?"

"Soda is very adult. Some refer to it as bubbly."

"Well then please pour me some bubbly, sir."

"Right away." Ethan fills our glasses with Coke. "Here's to a magnificent night."

"Cheers." We clink glasses. I've never felt so grownup.

"Any news on the new album?" I ask.

"We talk about me too much," Ethan says. "How are you doing with all this?"

"All this what?"

"The rock star girlfriend thing. Is it working for you?"

"Oh yeah." I slide closer to Ethan. "It's working."

"You're not overwhelmed?"

"The paparazzi can be a little scary. But then there are

nights like this with glitzy swag bags and major celeb sightings. So it all balances out."

"How's it going at school?"

"I miss you. So much."

"Sorry I'm not there for you more."

"It's okay. Being the world's biggest rock star is more important. But Miles and Reyna keep asking about you."

"I owe Miles a call."

"He really misses you. He doesn't like to show it, but he does."

"Have I turned into a horrible friend?"

"It's nothing a call won't fix."

"Okay, I'll call him. What else is going on with you?"

My idea for that cooking video series has been taking shape. I keep thinking about which recipes and techniques I want to share in the first few segments. But I'm not ready to tell Ethan about my idea yet. I don't want to share it with him until I have a solid plan.

"You know," I say. "Yoga. Cooking. College apps." It's weird that Ethan's not applying to colleges with me. I assumed we'd be navigating the whole process together. He's not even going to college.

"How's Gram?" he asks.

"Back to her old routine. Killing it at bingo. Baking up a storm. Having her back home is such a relief."

"Is she one hundred percent?"

"Totally. Her doctor said she kicked serious angioplasty butt."

"Good. You don't have to worry anymore."

"Now I'm just worrying about you."

"Why?"

"You have a million things to deal with. I don't know how you're doing it all. Aren't you exhausted?"

"Not when adrenaline and fear take over. They're a powerful upper combo."

"What are you afraid of?"

Ethan holds my hand between his. I love the way our hands fit together. Like he will always protect me.

"Sometimes I worry that it could all disappear," Ethan says. "You know how this business is. An artist is hot one day and forgotten the next."

"That could never happen to you."

"It could happen to anyone."

"Not you. Your fans love you for a reason. Not just because of how sexy you are or how strongly your music resonates with them or how your voice makes them melt. You're one of the best musicians ever. People will still be talking about you decades from now. Trust me. You've already made history and you're only eighteen. Imagine what you'll have accomplished by the time you're twenty-five."

Ethan brushes his hand against my cheek. He looks at me tenderly.

"You know how long I've been waiting for my dreams to come true," he says. "But it means so much more sharing everything with you. You're my angel, Sterling."

Ethan kisses me. It feels so good. The supercharged

electricity between us is more intense than ever. I lean back against the soft leather seat. Ethan puts a throw pillow under my head. He kisses me and kisses me like he can't get enough.

This is what true love feels like.

This is what ultimate happiness feels like.

This is what it's like to be with the boy every girl wants.

23

Watching Ethan rehearse is hot.

This week has been amazing. First the benefit packed with glitterati. Now I get to watch Ethan rehearse at the theater they rented in New York. All his backup dancers live here. So does his choreographer, stylist, and everyone else involved in developing a tour they promise will blow the roof off every single venue.

The crew is so nice. They keep coming over to where I'm sitting in the third row to say hi. They ask if I want a drink (I'm good). They ask if I want a snack (no, thanks). They ask what I think of the rehearsal (freaking amazing). They were rehearsing at a studio before this. But the tour is starting in two weeks. Everyone needs to see how it's coming together onstage.

Ethan is a natural. That's the only way to describe it. The way he's so comfortable with the choreo. The way he makes each song come alive. The way he owns the stage. He was born to do this. People are saying he's the next Michael Jackson. Ethan moves to the rhythm a lot like Michael did. It's like every cell of his body absorbs the music in such a soulful way that watching him dance is a transcendental experience.

"Night on Fire" involves pyrotechnics. The set is sensational. Fire jets burst when the lights are snapped off as the first chorus starts. Right when the flames burst, Ethan jumps from higher to lower risers on the stage. All these different levels are set up. They look like boxes glowing yellow, orange, and red. Ethan moves between them so smoothly you hardly even notice they're not connected. I'd be tripping over myself on the first jump.

After practicing "Night on Fire" four times, the director shouts for everyone to take a break. I head backstage to meet up with Ethan. I can't wait to tell him how hot he looked. Hotter than fire.

On my way to Ethan's dressing room, I hear Gage talking in a room I'm about to pass. Something about the tone of his voice makes me stop before the doorway and listen.

"We all started out on the same level," Gage is saying. "Now we're just called 'Ethan Cross'? That's bullshit. At least 'Ethan Cross and The Invincibles' acknowledged our existence. How did we go from practicing in Ethan's garage to Ethan being the only one people know?"

"They know us." Drew.

"No they don't." Stefan.

"The hardcore fans do." Drew.

"But it shouldn't be like that." Gage. "Look at Led Zeppelin. People don't only know Robert Plant. Jimmy Page is just as famous. They even know who John Bonham was."

"Hells yeah." Stefan.

"Who was on keys in Led Zeppelin?" Drew.

"John Paul Jones." Gage.

"I thought he played bass."

"He did. He's a multi-instrumentalist. He's also a composer and songwriter. Sound familiar?"

You can hear the resentment in Gage's voice. He's so jealous of Ethan. They probably all are. But Drew and Stefan are choosing to be mostly positive. I guess Gage is never going to be happy about Ethan's success. Which is a shame. Success for Ethan means success for the entire band. Why can't Gage see that?

"Are you comparing yourself to a member of one of the best bands ever?"

"I'm saying that I write songs, too. Our sound could seriously evolve if Ethan would respect that. I'm so tired of him calling the shots. We're all partners in this band. We should all have equal say."

I remember that band practice back in May when Gage asked Ethan about adding "Aluminum Rain" to the set list. Does he remember how Drew and Stefan agreed with Ethan?

How they said Gage's music isn't as strong as Ethan's?

Gage continues his rant. "Why does Ethan get all the attention? Why is he the only famous one here? Why him and not me?"

"You're not Neil Young," Drew says. "Get over it."

"You don't think I could be as successful as Ethan? Because I could. If I got the chance, I could."

"This *is* your chance. All of this. Right now. Which you would realize if you weren't so cynical."

"You don't think my songs are as good as Ethan's. Isn't that what you said? My music's not as strong as Ethan's and we should stick with what works?"

"Take it easy, man."

"Why are you always telling me to take it easy? Don't you have ambition? Am I the only one of us who wants more?"

"Of course we want more. But we appreciate what we have."

"Whatever. You don't get it." Gage's voice is getting louder, like he's walking toward the door. I skittle around the corner to take the other way to Ethan's dressing room. Ethan's not there. I sit on the floor outside to wait. While I'm waiting, I notice a cardboard sign on the wall across the hall.

KEEP THIS DOOR CLOSE AT ALL TIMES

There's no way I can ignore that glaring typo. Like, what, we're supposed to take the door off the hinges and carry it with us everywhere we go? I look around. No one else is in the hall. I whip a pen out of my bag and change *close* to *closed*. Then I sit back down before anyone can catch me. I'm such a typo terrorist. But I don't regret making the correction. I'm a typo terrorist with standards.

A roadie comes around the corner behind me.

"What are you?" he asks. "Some renegade copy editor?"

I look at him. I can't tell if he thinks I'm as abhorrent as I feel.

He just laughs. "There are some dumbasses around here."

Even though he's on my side, it hits me that I have to stop it with the correcting. I can see how obsessively correcting other people's ignorance could be considered offensive. What if someone else catches me and posts what a freak I am online? From now on, I have to assume that someone's always watching me. Maybe it's enough just to notice the typos exist. If I'm noticing, I still care.

"Hey!" Ethan swoops down to give me a kiss. "Sorry, I'm all sweaty."

"That's okay." I was going to tell Ethan what Gage said. But it's probably better not to. Ethan would get stressed out and there'd be even more tension. I don't want anything to get in the way of a phenomenal tour.

"What do you think so far?" he asks.

"It's amazing. You're amazing."

He kisses me again. "Did you like the fire?"

"Of course. But you were hotter than the fire."

Ethan's eyes burn into mine. I love it when he looks at me

that way. Like he's starving in the desert and I'm an ice-cream sundae.

"Come in for a minute," he says.

We go into his dressing room. Right before Ethan closes the door behind us, the roadie catches my eye from across the hall.

He salutes me.

24

I couldn't have asked for a better New Year's Eve. Ethan did an early acoustic show at a small venue in New York. The audience mainly consisted of contest winners. The show streamed live and will be rebroadcast on MTV later tonight. They set Ethan up with a gorgeous penthouse at the W Times Square. I'm totally staying with him. My mom thinks I'm sleeping over at Georgia's.

We have the whole night to ourselves.

The last time we had a night together like this, just the two of us to do whatever we wanted, was last summer. I remember that one night like it was yesterday. Mom was away. Ethan told his parents he was sleeping over at Drew's. We had the best time doing nothing. We found a quiet dock to lie back on and watch the stars. We were surrounded by water, the soothing night folding us into darkness. Fireflies glimmered around us. We went back to my place. I made my extra-buttery movie popcorn and we watched *(500) Days of Summer*.

Then we went to my room. It wasn't the first night Ethan slept over. But the night was so magical it felt like the first time.

Tonight feels like the first time all over again.

"I like your dress," Ethan says.

"Thanks."

"It's sparkly. Like you."

"You think I'm sparkly?"

"Always." He leans across the table to kiss me. I can feel people looking at us even with my eyes closed. But for the first time since people started recognizing Ethan, I don't care. Tonight is about us. Tonight we're the only thing that matters.

People from my cooking class were freaking out when I told them I'd be going to Serendipity on New Year's Eve. Everyone knows Serendipity has the best frozen hot chocolate ever. I found the recipe online last year and whipped up a pitcher. Even though it was seriously delicious, I couldn't wait to taste the real thing. When Ethan asked where I wanted to go for New Year's, I jumped at the chance to come here. It's not only about the food. Serendipity is shimmering with decorations and winter floral arrangements and thousands of twinkling Christmas lights. The place is packed with other couples and groups of friends appreciating how special it is to be here on New Year's. They probably made reservations months ago.

The only reason Zeke was able to get a reservation for us a few days ago is because of Ethan.

We can't decide what else to order.

"Dude," Ethan says. "What's this Golden Opulence Sundae?"

"Where?"

"Down at the bottom."

"Oh my god. *A thousand dollars?* For a sundae?"

"That's one rich sundae."

"It has edible gold leaf. Oh, and you get to take the crystal goblet home."

"Want to order it?"

"Are you insane?"

"Why not? It's a special occasion."

Ethan has told me a little about how much he's making. He doesn't like to talk about it. From what he's told me, I know he could totally afford the sundae. Or even a hundred sundaes.

"That sundae is outrageous," I say. "Anyway, it says you need to order it forty-eight hours in advance."

"At least we still have the Vesuvius."

"What's that?"

"I think it's what those guys are having." Ethan glances at the table next to ours. A giddy twentysomething couple is sharing an enormous piece of cheesecake. The slice is so big it's more like a whole cake. It's so tremendous that the cake even has straws sticking out of it.

"Cake requiring straws?" I say. "I need that recipe."

"Want to order it?"

"Too intimidating. Let's go with the Strawberry Fields Sundae."

"Done." Ethan smacks down the menu. "This place is incredible."

We look around in awe, pointing out our favorite details. A rowdy table of girls in the corner totally knows who Ethan is. A few of them have their phones out. They keep looking over here. They're spazzing in that way where you're trying to appear calm but you aren't fooling anyone. Even the air molecules around their table are twanging with excitement.

Our waiter comes by. Ethan orders the Strawberry Fields.

"Are those girls bothering you?" the waiter asks. He indicates the rowdy table with a flick of his wrist.

"Not at all." Ethan smiles at me. "We're just enjoying being here."

"Exquisite, isn't it?" the waiter says.

"It really is," I agree.

"Just let me know if you need anything. And um . . . not to get all fangirl on you? But I cannot *wait* for your show at the Garden. I scored floor seats!"

"Thanks," Ethan says. "I'm already stoked."

"It'll be a night on fire, burning with desire. Please tell me I did not just say that. *Oh*-kay, I'll be back with your sundae."

"What's it like to have everyone in the world love you?" I wonder.

"Nothing compared to having you love me."

Melting. At. Serendipity.

Ethan reaches for my hand across the table. "I wish it

could always be like this. Sorry I've been so busy."

"You have nothing to apologize for. Your biggest dreams are becoming reality. That's the most important thing."

"Nothing is more important than us."

Being with Ethan makes me happier than anything else ever could. I don't even care that people are watching me swoon over my boyfriend.

"Um. Excuse me?" One of the girls from the rowdy table is standing at ours.

"Hi," Ethan says.

"Can I just say we love you? We're all huge fans. Like, *huge*."

"Thanks."

"Oh my god, we love you so much!"

"Where are you girls from?"

"Here. No, not *here*, not like we live in a restaurant, ha! We're from the Upper West."

"Awesome."

"Could you come over and take pictures with us? Sorry to interrupt . . ." Her eyes slide over me.

"Of course. Sterling doesn't mind." Ethan flashes me his best rock star smile. My stomach sinks. I force my mouth to smile back. This was supposed to be our night. Just the two of us blocking out the rest of the world. I wish he didn't want to let anyone else in.

Sitting alone at Serendipity on New Year's Eve? Not so fun.

"Here you go!" the waiter announces. "Our finest Strawberry Fields." He places the sundae at the center of the table with a flourish. "Where's your man?"

I gesture to the table of squealing fangirls in the corner. Ethan is smiling and posing for pictures as the girls take turns capturing what will undoubtedly be one of the best moments of their lives.

"A rock star's work is never done," the waiter singsongs. He zips off to a table of three beaming couples.

I pick up one of the ice-cream spoons. We always take our first bites of dessert together. But Ethan's talking with those fans like I'm not even here.

The girl at the table next to ours was smiling at us when we were holding hands across the table. Now she throws me a pity glance.

I dig my spoon into the sundae. Part of me wants to march over there and yank Ethan back. But the rational part knows Ethan is just doing his thing. He's so dedicated to his fans. I don't want to ruin our night with drama. So I swallow my feelings along with the melting ice cream.

After Serendipity, a car is waiting for us out front. We have to squeeze between the line of people waiting for tables and a glass case featuring Serendipity merchandise.

"Do you want a shirt?" Ethan asks.

Two girls whip out their phones and point them at Ethan. Other people in line are starting to stare.

"That's okay," I say. "We should go."

The car takes us to our hotel. We don't have that far to go, but traffic is moving at a glacial pace with the Times Square New Year's crowds. I people-watch out the window and wonder what it would be like to live in such a vibrant city. I'd probably go out every night if I lived here.

Back at our Extreme WOW Suite, I turn on the huge TV. It's wild to be watching the same New Year's celebration that's happening below us. There's less than fifteen minutes to go.

Ethan checks the acoustic show rebroadcast online to see how it looks. Then he checks his fan page. Someone posted a picture of us at Serendipity. It already has over five thousand likes.

"I bet it was those girls in the corner," I say.

"Oh yeah, it had to be. See how Santa's sleigh is behind us?"

"Cute picture." I go over to the gift basket the production company sent. We tore into it the second we got to the room before the show. It's sitting on a coffee table between two plush armchairs in front of an enormous picture window. Manhattan glows below us. Times Square is lit up so brightly it looks like daytime. Throngs of people are bunched together to watch the ball drop. Zeke told Ethan he should stay at a downtown hotel away from the crowds. But Ethan wanted to see how New Year's Eve in Times Square looked from the fifty-seventh floor.

I take out a chocolate-covered strawberry.

"You're eating more chocolate?" Ethan says. "How is that even possible?"

"I'm a girl. We like our chocolate."

"You're lucky. If my trainer knew what we just ate, he'd kill me."

"It's New Year's Eve. Don't you get a night off on New Year's Eve?"

"Only on the DL." Ethan comes up behind me and puts his hands on my waist. "Good strawberry?"

"*So* good." I lean back against him. We watch the celebration below. I watch us reflected in the glass, watching everyone else. Images of us flash behind my eyes as the countdown begins on TV.

"Ten . . . nine . . . eight . . ."

Ethan asking me out for the first time "I like your streak" taking me to that show at The Space performing at The Space when it was already so obvious he was going to be a major rock star—

". . . seven . . . six . . . five . . ."

—in Ethan's room last summer sitting on his lap with my hair still wet from the pool kissing him hearing his first single on the radio and freaking out together Ethan getting signed for a huge second album Forever going straight to number one—

"four . . . three . . ."

—those fangirls obsessing over Ethan at this first big solo show sitting on Ethan's porch while he bounces a basketball in the orange sunlight paparazzi stalking us at the Notch Ethan bowling in the fog our supercharged electricity in the stretch limo hooking up in his dressing room at rehearsal when he only had five minutes—

". . . two . . . one . . . Happy New Year!"

"Remember this night when we're apart," Ethan says. "Remember how much I love you."

25

How weird is it that so many of the things defining my life now first started happening just a few months ago? Pictures of Ethan and me are in all the entertainment magazines, online, and on TV. Paparazzi stalk us constantly. Ethan's songs are always playing. They're playing on the radio, in stores, in restaurants, in cars, and on the devices of millions of fans.

Ethan Cross is everywhere.

There's definitely love for him here in Miami. I flew down to watch his tour kick off. Then I'll be riding the tour bus with him to Orlando. Mom thought missing a few extra days of school right after the break would be the least disruptive. I'll get to join Ethan again in California and New York. Maybe a few other cities if Mom lets me go.

South Beach is really interesting. There's a lot of history here, but not in a boring way. This is the art deco district. Everywhere you look there are buildings with deco fonts from the thirties, balconies with squiggly edges, portholes along walls, and bright pastel colors. Everything is lit with neon lights. I had no idea Miami was this cool.

We're staying at a hotel so swanky it's called The Hotel. The whole crew is staying here. Everyone is being supersweet to me. I feel bad that I can't remember all of their names. Ethan had to rehearse after we checked in. The first thing I did was change into a bikini and run down to the infinity pool. Ethan's stylist was already down there. Aixa was saving the lounge chair next to her for me like she somehow knew I would show up. Aixa is one of those people who is so classy she scares me. But now that we've talked and lounged and read magazines together, I feel way more comfortable around her. How awesome is it that we could lay out by the pool in January? Seventy-five degrees is my kind of winter. I never want to leave this hotel. Our suite probably isn't as big as most of the other hotel rooms on tour will be, but it has an ocean-front balcony. And it's impeccably designed. Boutique hotels are all about the details.

I'm admiring the deco trim in the lobby when a group of three girls plunges through the revolving doors in a burst of laughter. They have enough luggage for a year. A porter whisks over to them and starts arranging their bags on a cart.

"If he were any hotter, he'd be on fire," a tall girl in plat-form wedges proclaims.

"Where were you the first time you heard 'Night on Fire'?" a short girl with an I ♥ LIFE tank top asks.

"Ordering fro-yo. Half peanut butter, half marshmallow, with bananas and chocolate syrup. I'll never forget it."

Gram would get a kick out of the peanut butter marshmallow banana fro-yo. That's probably what Elvis would have.

"I was driving home from school," the short girl says. "I could not stop screaming. I almost hit a stop sign."

"You were texting me from your *car*?" the third girl says. "Do you know how dangerous that is?"

"What was I supposed to do? Not tell you Ethan was on the radio?"

"You could have pulled over."

"Ladies," Platform Wedges says. "Let's remember why we're here. We're the ones who discovered Ethan. How many other fans here for this show can say they saw him at The Space? Before he was even headlining?"

"Zero," I ♥ LIFE confirms.

"Exactly. We freaking *rule*."

Normally I would let this kind of manic chatter roll right off me. But now I shoot the girls a look. Why does every single fan have to be so possessive of Ethan? It's like they're all competing against one another to claim ownership of him. Ethan's not an object. He's a real person. With a real girlfriend.

If these girls only knew they were staying at the same hotel as Ethan. They'd take turns sleeping so one of them could always be on the lookout in the lobby.

A familiar boy comes up to me. I recognize his shaggy,

dark hair and gray eyes, but I can't remember where I've seen him before.

"You into art deco?" he asks.

"I'm getting into it. The designs are gorgeous."

"There's a deco tour of South Beach. Let me know if you're interested."

"Thanks. Have you taken it?"

"Don't need to. I used to live here."

"Sweet. You grew up here, or . . . ?"

"Not exactly."

I wait for him to explain. He doesn't.

"This is going to sound horrible, but I can't remember where we met," I admit.

"I'm Damien. A roadie with the tour? I saw you—"

"—backstage at rehearsals, right! Sorry, I've been meeting so many people."

"No worries. I was going to introduce myself that day. Only you were . . . busy."

The memory of Damien saluting me as Ethan closed his dressing room door makes me blush.

"I'm Sterling. Nice to officially meet you."

"You, too." Damien looks around the lobby. "Sick hotel, huh? This tour's going to rock. We usually don't get to stay at places this nice. If Ethan hadn't insisted the crew stay where he does, we'd be at the Holiday Inn."

"How long have you been a roadie?"

"Three years."

Damien doesn't look that much older than me. I guess he didn't go to college.

"Do you like it?" I ask.

"I love being on the road."

"It seems like it would be fun for a while. But I don't think I could travel all the time. Don't you get homesick?"

"Never. The thought of settling down depresses me. It's like once you grow roots somewhere, you become entrenched in routine. You get chained to some small life you build in your tiny corner of the world. Behind walls that trap your suffering and smother your instincts. Life should be more than coming home every night to the same sad place. It all relates to my theory of higher intelligence."

"Which is?"

"What if there's a form of intelligence higher than humans? Maybe we are to them what pets are to us. How are our lives that much different from hamsters? They're comforted by the routine of running in their wheel. They're like us, doing the same things day after day, mindlessly sticking to the familiarity of our little world because we're afraid of what exists beyond the walls we've built."

Two other guys from the tour pass by us on their way out. Damien nods at them.

"I mean, think about it," he goes on. "We watch our cats and dogs perform their little rituals. They come running for food on cue when they hear the rustle of the bag or the whir of the can opener. Dogs go ballistic at the door when they hear keys jangling. We think their lives are so simple. But aren't our lives just as basic, only on a larger scale? What if some higher intelligence is watching us the same way? When we wonder about things that could exist beyond what we know, we're like every dog jumping and barking at the door, dying to get out. Most people wake up at the same time, go to the same job, come home to the same dinners, watch the same shows. There has to be more to life than that. It would be freaking depressing if there wasn't, you know?"

Damien just gave me so much to think about I don't even know where to start. I kind of like routine. But I also like adventure. What would it be like to travel for a living? To have no one place to call home?

"What about people who like their lives?" I say. "Not everyone is unhappy."

"It's sad how unhappy the majority of people are. But they stay at jobs they hate and in marriages that aren't working because they're afraid to make a change. They don't understand that life has to change in order to get better. They're settling for mediocrity out of fear. I don't want to be like that. I want to find a better way."

"I get what you're saying," I tell him. "If you're not happy, what's the point?"

"Exactly." Damien looks at me with those soulful, gray eyes. Now I can see more in them than depth. There's also loneliness.

"So are you excited for tonight?" I ask, attempting to

lighten the mood. "Or is opening night just another gig for you by now?"

"The energy is exciting. Opening and closing nights are the most charged."

"I'm so happy I get to be there."

"Are you going to watch from backstage?"

"Zeke gave me a front row center seat. He kept asking if I was sure I wanted to be up front in the limelight. As if anyone will even notice me." This is Ethan's first show of the tour at a major sold-out venue. I have to see what it looks like from the floor.

"Trust me," Damien says. "They're noticing."

He looks at me. I recognize the intensity of his look.

"Well . . . I should get ready," I say. "You're going over soon, right?"

"Yeah. See you there."

"See you." Walking back to the elevators, I wonder if I read Damien's look right. Maybe not. Maybe he just needed someone to talk to.

The show is beyond amazing. When Ethan comes out onstage, the surge of screaming from the crowd makes my pulse race. The energy of twelve thousand fans oscillates all around me. I'm so close to the stage that the projection screens are undecipherable dots of color. The only reason I know what's showing on them is that I was here for rehearsal. Videos of Ethan practicing guitar in elementary school and performing in talent shows in high school play in my mind. His mom showed me hours of recordings when she was narrowing down possible video clips for the tour. I love that she kept all of them. These screaming fans obviously love it, too.

Being this close is a rush. It's just me and Ethan with no one else in between. I can see the sweat dripping down his face. His sneaker twitching as he counts the beat to "Now and Forever." The outline of the *mati* in his pocket. When he finds me in the front row and smiles at me, he makes me feel like I'm the only one here.

I take some pictures. The view is perfect. I snap an excellent one of Ethan jumping from a riser, flames blazing behind him. The effects look a million times more impressive now. The crowd is singing along to every word. Every word that Ethan wrote, hoping someday they would be embedded in the minds of his fans.

At this moment, with the crowd screaming and the music resonating and the rich sounds of Ethan's voice filling my heart, there are no words to describe how happy I am for him. He always knew that dreaming big would lead him here. He envisioned all of this so long ago. Then he made it happen. Ethan Cross never gave up.

Ethan Cross proves that dreams do come true.

26

Life on the road is fun. At least, life on the road from Miami to Orlando in Ethan's double-decker tour bus is fun. This tour bus is like a huge, tricked-out trailer. There's a kitchen against the wall behind the driver's area. The living room extends from the front door to the office. A black leather sectional couch in a U-shape takes up most of the living room. A dining table and chairs are set up next to the kitchen. There's a bathroom downstairs and another bathroom and four bedrooms upstairs. Except for the highway views and constant motion, the bus totally feels like an apartment.

The band and crew are riding in other buses. Ethan's bus is just us, his vocal coach Liz, Zeke, and two drivers who switch on and off. Ethan and I have bunk beds in the bedroom we're sharing. We're sitting on the big stretch of couch that runs along one side of the living room, strategizing how Ethan will sneak into my bed tonight.

"We should wait until everyone's asleep," I say.

"Zeke never sleeps. The man is a beast. He won't care anyway. He knows we hook up."

"Ssshh!" I hiss as Liz passes us on her way to the kitchen.

"We don't have to be quiet. I'm telling you. They don't care."

"Excuse me, but I care."

"Why?"

"Because it's embarrassing."

"It's embarrassing for you to be with me?"

"No! It's embarrassing that they know."

"Of course they know. Everyone knows."

"So you don't care if everyone knows you'll be sneaking into my bed?"

Ethan pulls me onto his lap. "I'd be crazy not to want people to know I'm sneaking into a gorgeous girl's bed."

I giggle. Liz walks by with a granola bar. She pretends not to notice I'm draped all over her client.

"Hey, Liz," Ethan says. "How's it going?"

"You have half an hour," Liz says ominously. She retreats to her room.

"What happens in half an hour?" I ask.

"You get tickled."

"No tickling."

"In half an hour? You'd rather be tickled now?"

"No!"

"I think you might." Ethan wiggles his fingers at me.

I scream and spring off his lap. Zeke pokes his head out of the office, covering his mouthpiece.

"Simmer down, kids," he says. "I'm on a conference call."

"You heard the man," Ethan tells me. "Simmer down."

"You started it."

"Only because you said you wanted to get tickled."

"I did not!"

"That's not how I remember it."

"I asked you what happens in half an hour."

"Oh. Lessons."

"Crazy how you're working all the time. Even on the bus."

"Gotta keep the instrument tuned."

"I wonder if the guys are having this much fun on their bus."

"They might be if Gage wasn't complaining all the time."

"He told you?"

"Told me what?"

"About how he's . . . you know. Not happy."

"Gage is unhappy?" Ethan's voice drips with sarcasm. "In other news, the sun is hot."

"Doesn't it make you feel bad, though? I mean, you *are* the one getting all the attention. Maybe there's something you could do to help him."

"Like what? Become huge so he gets more attention than most artists dream of in a lifetime? Oh, wait. I already did that."

"What about if you added 'Aluminum Rain' to the set list? You could—"

"Look," Ethan interrupts. "I appreciate what you're doing here? But you don't understand. This is way more complicated than throwing Gage a bone. I'll take care of it." Ethan picks up his phone to check messages. End of discussion.

My stomach drops. Why did Ethan have to shut me down like that? I was just trying to help. But it's like he thought I was insulting his judgment or something.

Ethan's phone rings. His phone has been blowing up. This is the longest conversation we've had without his phone or a crew member interrupting us since before the tour.

"Hey, Sydney," he says.

Sydney is like a whole other sister now. She's gradually come to admire Ethan's passion and the amazing life he's creating. Everyone treating her like rock star royalty at school probably helped to improve her attitude.

"Did you send it?" Ethan is asking Sydney. He checks his screen. There's a picture of Sydney and two of her friends. They're all wearing *mati* necklaces. Ethan said in an interview how the *mati* his grandfather gave him is his lucky charm that he puts in his pocket before every show. The video went viral a few weeks ago. I saw a bunch of girls at the Miami show last night wearing *mati* jewelry—necklaces, rings, bracelets. One girl painted a *mati* on a white tee in dark blue and light blue with *Ethan Cross* circling around it in black. I even saw a picture posted on Ethan's fan page of a girl making heart hands with a *mati* tattooed to the back of her hand.

Zeke bursts out of the office. Zeke is always bursting into and out of rooms. Being fueled by the five cups of coffee he's compelled to drink before noon every day helps him to maintain a perpetually wired state.

"What was that?" he fires at Ethan.

"What was what?"

"All that screaming while I was on a conference call?"

"Sorry," I say. "It was my fault."

"No, it was Ethan's fault," Zeke insists. "He knows better than to get you all worked up when I'm conducting business ten feet away."

"Okay, Dad," Ethan says. "Jeez. Overreact much?"

"Hey. I'm on the grind for you twenty-four seven. Your career was built from the ground up by me. Maybe you need me to act like a father figure to straighten you out. Legendary producers don't want to hear kids screaming in the background when they're trying to negotiate a deal."

"I'm not a kid. I can take care of myself."

"No, you *are* a kid. You need to do what I say. I know what's best for you. Like when I tell you not to stay up so late, you need to get to bed earlier. You looked like crap for that early photo shoot."

"How was I supposed to know they moved the time up?"

"Schedules change all the time. You know this. You have to be ready in the morning for anything. The day can take a million different turns. I want you looking polished and professional by eight every morning." Zeke angles his head toward his mouthpiece. He does this when he's getting a call. Then he glances at his phone to see who's calling. "Go for Zeke." He bursts back into the office, slamming the door behind him.

"As if I don't already have one disappointed dad," Ethan mumbles. Ethan doesn't like to show how much it bothers him when Zeke gets harsh. But I know Zeke's approach can push Ethan's buttons.

I lie down on the couch, using Ethan's lap as a pillow. Exhausted doesn't even begin to describe me. We had so much adrenaline pumping after the show last night that we couldn't sleep. We stayed up in Ethan's room at the hotel until it got light out.

That's being on tour. Staying up late. Always moving. Constant excitement. Now I get what Damien was saying about life on the road. How he loves the adventure. How he's searching for a better way. How he won't settle for anything less than what he's determined to find.

It's the last thought I have before falling asleep.

27

Georgia is in love.

And she'll do anything to make Kurt admit he loves her, too.

"He's probably scared," Georgia rationalizes. "Boys are all scared of commitment. It's a documented fact."

I'm not sure that's why Kurt doesn't want to be exclusive. Georgia shouldn't have to convince him to be her boyfriend. She shouldn't be waiting for him to say "I love you" three weeks after she said it. If someone truly loved you, wouldn't they want to make sure you knew it?

"What are boys so afraid of?" Georgia says. "Sharing their feelings? Opening up to another person? Being vulnerable? Telling their secrets to someone else?"

"All of the above?" I say. I don't say what I'm really thinking. Which is that Kurt seems to be afraid of being stuck with Georgia in case someone better comes along.

"You're so lucky to have Ethan. He's like the only mature boy I know." Georgia looks around at the boys loping by our bench in the courtyard with disdain. School just ended. We watch boys going to their lockers and practice and activities. "Children. All of them."

I wish there were some way to help Georgia. But when you're in love, you can't hear anyone who dares trying to convince you that your object of desire might not be worth your time.

"Should I give Kurt an ultimatum? Either he commits or it's over?"

"An ultimatum probably isn't the best way to start an official relationship." I offer Georgia my pack of Chuckles. She shakes her head. "Wouldn't it be better if he *wants* to commit?"

"He does want to. Deep down. He just doesn't know it yet."

I shove a yellow Chuckle in my mouth before I say something she doesn't want to hear. Reyna and Miles come up to our bench.

"Hey, Sterling," Reyna says. "How's it going?"

"Good." I haven't really talked to Reyna or Miles since Ethan left school. We don't even sit together at lunch anymore. "How are you guys?"

"Crazy busy," Miles says. "I have no free time with basketball and AP Bio."

"Ahem," Reyna interjects.

"And with keeping this one happy."

"You know it."

"So yeah. Crazy busy."

"I heard you went on part of Ethan's tour," Reyna tells me. "How was it?"

"Awesome."

"How's he doing? We haven't heard from him in forever."

"He's good. Loving the tour. I told him to call you guys."

"No worries," Miles says. "I have a lot going on. It's not like I've had time to catch up with him."

"Tell him we said hey?" Reyna says.

"Of course."

"See you around."

I wonder how many other friends Ethan's not talking to. I mean, I get it, his schedule is insane. But it's not like him to lose touch with his friends. They were always so important to him before.

Kids ask me about Ethan all the time. People I don't even know are constantly hounding me for information. And not just at school. Random people come up to me wherever I go. Or they stare at me and pretend they're not. They pretend they don't want to ask whatever they're dying to know. The attention is fun. Socializing is my thing. It makes me feel special to be the only person in the world who knows Ethan as well as I do. The only person who can answer their questions. But sometimes it's annoying. There are creepers and haters. People feel the need to tell me all about the music they're working on. They ask if I could pass demos along to Ethan. As if he's a producer. He's trying to make it just like they are. Don't they get that?

I can't remember the last time someone talked to me without asking about Ethan.

"So what should I do?" Georgia asks.

"About what?"

"Um. Kurt? The boy we've been talking about this whole time? Well. Not this *whole* time."

"Are you mad that they were asking about Ethan?"

"Why would I be mad? I was just trying to get advice from my best friend. Whatever."

"Sorry about that. You know how it's been."

"Yeah. I know."

Awkward silence.

"Do you still want my advice?" I ask.

Georgia nods.

"Don't settle. The right boy for you will adore you. He'll make it very clear how he feels about you. You won't have to wonder if he wants to be your boyfriend. It will just happen naturally."

"You don't think Kurt is the right boy for me?"

"I didn't say that."

"Yeah. You kind of did." Georgia jumps up and grabs her bag. "I have to go."

"No, wait. I'm sorry I said that. I didn't mean—"

"Just forget it." Georgia storms off.

Crap. I knew I was going to say something she didn't want to hear.

I call Georgia later that night.

"Are you still mad at me?" I ask.

"I'm not mad. I'm . . . frustrated. I have a ton of homework and no motivation to do any of it."

"Look. I'm sorry you're going through all this drama with Kurt. I'm here if you want to talk about it some more."

"I wanted to talk about it when you were sitting next to me. But I guess that was too much to ask."

"I'm your best friend. I'm always here for you."

"Except when you're not."

"You're mad I went to see Ethan? That was—"

"No. It's not . . . it doesn't matter. I have to go." Georgia hangs up before I can find out what's wrong.

Things have been strained with us for a while. Sometimes it feels like our friendship is fading away. Which sucks because I don't even know what I did wrong. And Georgia won't tell me. I keep reaching out to her. But she keeps not wanting to talk.

I wish I knew how to fix this.

28

The adrenaline rush of having gone on tour with Ethan has worn off. I feel like I've been run over by a truck. The weather isn't helping. It's cold and dreary out. Which, news flash, it's the end of January. But it feels like winter will never end. Snow is blowing in sideways. The drab gray sky is more effective than a sleeping pill. All I want to do is take a big nap.

Except I can't take a nap. The amount of homework my teachers slammed me with is absurd. Talking to Ethan will give me the jolt I need. But my call goes straight to voice mail.

Ethan is unavailable. Again.

I check Ethan's fan page to see if he posted any updates today. Unlike with his friends, he's awesome about staying in touch with his fans. Even when he's super busy. There's a new picture from the show in Portland two nights ago. There's a post from Ethan asking Seattle if they're ready for tonight. And there's a new behind-the-scenes video from rehearsals. It already has 11,250 comments. I scroll through some of them, smiling at how much love Ethan's fans have for him.

Then I see this:

> Why is Ethan with Sterling anyway?? She's not even that pretty.

Now I feel like I've been run over by a truck and then slapped upside the head. Why would someone feel the need to post that?

Tears sting my eyes. Normally I'd brush off nasty comments. But I've been feeling extra sensitive about the way I look. Part of the reason Ethan is a rock star is that he looks like a rock star. Do I look like a rock star's girlfriend? Not at all. Every time I see a picture of us in a magazine or on TV or online, I cringe at how lacking I am. Ethan could totally be with the most gorgeous movie star and they'd look like the perfect couple.

A message pops up on my screen. From Damien.

> Corrected any good typos lately?

> I'm taking a break. Too cold to notice. You?

> No one schools a sign like you do. I'll leave the improvements in your capable hands. What are you doing?

Drowning in a sea of misery.

Nasty comment online?

How did you know?

People are harsh. I really hate them sometimes.

I shouldn't be so sensitive. I don't know why I'm letting it bother me.

Feel like talking?

That's okay. You must be busy.

On break. Call me at 305.555.0189.

The truth is, I'm dying to talk to someone. Georgia has been avoiding me. I try Ethan again and get his voice mail. So I call Damien.

He picks up on the first ring. "Hey."

"Hey. Thanks for talking."

"No problem. What did the dumbass say?"

"She said I'm not pretty enough to be with Ethan."

"Not everyone has the gift of sight."

"You're sweet, but—"

"She obviously has impaired vision. Have you looked in the mirror? You're a beautiful girl."

Fortunately Damien can't see me blushing over the phone.

"Want me to have the comment deleted?" he asks.

"We should leave it. Deleting it would just make her retaliate with something meaner. Like anyone has to remind me of how lacking I am. I know I'm not a celeb. I know I'm not perfect. Ethan could have any girl he wants. I'm already afraid he's going to leave me for some supermodel. So why do people feel the need to remind me that he could do better?"

"First of all, you're insane. You're equating celebrity status with perfection. Do you have any idea how broken most of them are? The underlying reason they're driven to chase fame is to compensate for everything missing in their lives. A lot is missing if they can't be happy unless the whole world loves them."

"But those girls are—"

"I'm not done."

"Sorry."

"Did you hear the part where I said you're beautiful?"

"Not really."

"Why not?"

"Because nasty comments like this one make me feel ugly. Because every time I see a picture of us together, all I can see are my flaws. Ethan looks like a rock star and I look like . . . a wannabe rock star's girlfriend."

"No, you *are* a rock star's girlfriend. You're the girlfriend of one of the hottest musicians in the world. If Ethan can have any girl he wants—which I don't believe, by the way—and he chooses to be with you, what does that tell you?"

"That I'm lucky we were together before he got famous?"

"What makes you think he isn't the lucky one? Are you even aware of how many guys would kill to be with you?"

I snort.

"Ever notice how the guys in the band look at you? They all want to be Ethan. They all want to be with you. You're the icing on the cake."

All I hear is the word *cake*. Now I want cake. Eating cake is my go-to remedy for alleviating depression.

"Trust me," Damien says. "Ethan's the lucky one."

The way Damien says it, I almost believe him.

29

Did I really just finish my last college application?

Yes. I totally just did.

This last app was for one of my safeties. My top three choices are Columbia, Princeton, and the University of Vermont, all of which have excellent English departments. My reluctance to take school seriously until recently will most likely prevent my acceptance to Columbia or Princeton. But the college advisor says that my chances are good for the University of Vermont.

The bell rings before I can fully appreciate the sensation of being done. It feels like I've been filling out forms and writing essays and gathering paperwork for years instead of three months. I make my way from the guidance office to class in a haze. The guidance counselor gave me the last letter I needed to include with my final app. I've done everything I possibly can to get into a good college. Now I just have to wait and see.

"Hey, Sterling!" One of the most popular seniors says hi to me in the hall every time she sees me now. She started being nice to me right after Ethan blew up. She hasn't asked me for tickets or swag or anything. It's more like she suddenly noticed I was a person.

I smile at her as we pass in the hall. Her friends beam radiant smiles back at me.

People are definitely treating me differently. I've always been a social person. I have lots of friends at school. But I'm getting way more attention now. Other kids are going out of their way to say hi to me. My teachers seem nicer. And it's not only at school. People stop to ask me about Ethan everywhere. Even Gram's friends drilled me about him when I dropped in on bingo night. Everyone in my yoga class watches me now. Their eyes are on me the second I get to the studio. I pretend not to notice as I set up my mat and fidget with my water bottle. But I secretly like the attention. What can I say? Classic extroverts like me are attention whores.

After school, I run home to work on my cooking video series. I've been trying to decide which ideas to use for my first video. I want to hook viewers right away so they come back for more. But what if they don't think I'm interesting enough? What if I'm the only one who geeks out over culinary dorktasticness?

There's an OXO strawberry huller I want to feature in the

first video. I bought it a few days ago at Bed and Bath. At first I was worried that it's really hard to find good strawberries in February. The hothouse ones generally look okay, but they taste like paper. Then I realized that no one has to eat them. I'm so used to cooking for people that I completely forgot I'd only be showing viewers how to prepare food, not serving it. The strawberry huller is a go.

Or not. There's an excellent mac and cheese recipe I just found online. With the crumbly topping and everything. Who can resist three kinds of cheeses? And not just any cheeses. The secret to an exceptional mac and cheese (other than whisking the melted butter, flour, and milk correctly) is to use only the best cheese. You wouldn't want to spend an hour preparing mac and cheese from scratch and then obliterate your time commitment by dumping in discount cheese. That would be a travesty.

People need to know this. I want to be the one to tell them.

There's also my signature frappé recipe I'm dying to feature. And an au gratin dish I've perfected that's to die. So much to share. So little time in a video that should be kept under five minutes if I have any hope of people watching it.

I know just who to call for a second opinion.

"Hey," Damien answers. "I was just thinking about you."

"Really?"

"Yeah. I was wondering if you've realized that nasty comment was bogus."

"Pretty much. I mean, it's always going to hurt to read

stuff like that. But I know I shouldn't let the haters get to me."

"That's what I wanted to hear."

"The terrorists cannot win."

"Preach it, girl."

"So I'm working on some video series development. I could really use your insight." I tell Damien all about my ideas. "Which one do you think I should start with?"

"Hmm. If it were me, I would probably lead with the mac and cheese. A crowd pleaser is always a sure thing."

"You're right. Thank you."

"Anytime."

I knew Damien would know the best way to begin. Now it's up to me to get over my fear of more hater trauma. Telling Damien I shouldn't let them bother me and getting to a place where they actually don't bother me are two totally different things.

30

[12,723,554 FOLLOWERS]

Ethan is back home for two days. Then I'm flying to California with him to go to his Los Angeles show. We're even getting some alone time. Which we haven't had in forever.

I almost forgot what it feels like to be this happy.

Not even the screaming fans at this meet-and-greet can bring me down. Five fans won a contest to meet Ethan at a studio in New Haven before taping some promos for his upcoming appearance on *Ellen*. Each of them was allowed to bring a friend. Ethan is surrounded by ten trembling girls who look like they're about to either faint, throw up, or burst out crying. Two of them have *mati* bracelets halfway up their arm. Three others are wearing Forever Tour concert tees.

"Do they have enough bracelets?" Georgia inquires about the *mati* girls. From where we're sitting in these tall director's chairs, we have a good view of everyone swarming Ethan in front of the stage. Georgia loves *Ellen*. Even though we're not on set, she really wanted to be here. She's counting it as being one degree from Ellen DeGeneres.

"Doubtful," I say. "I can still see skin."

"You're right. Where's the dedication?"

The girls are taking pictures with Ethan. He takes the time to connect with each one of them. He even tells the girls to check their pictures to make sure they came out okay. He retakes the ones that didn't.

I see hunger in their eyes. Desire. They know Ethan has a girlfriend. They know his girlfriend is sitting right here. But they don't care. They would get with him in a second. Even if it meant he'd be cheating on me.

After the taping, I wait in Ethan's dressing room for him to wrap it up. Georgia comes back from the bathroom. She's all flushed.

"Are you okay?" I ask.

"Totally," Georgia says, breathless. She's carrying some 8-by-10 glossy photos of Ethan.

"What just happened?"

"Nothing. Ethan gave me some signed pictures."

"For who?"

"My friends."

"Which friends?"

"Just . . . some girls from school."

"Who?"

Georgia can't even look at me. "Kelsey, Markita, and Ravyne."

"What? Why?" Georgia knows I hate it when she bothers Ethan for signed swag. Or asks me to bother him. I can't believe she went behind my back. And for those bitches? What the hell?

"They're being a lot nicer to me. Kelsey is friends with Kurt. She said she'd talk to him for me." Georgia is fussing with her coat and bag. She still can't look at me. "Anyway. Ethan didn't even mind. It's no big deal."

"No big deal? Since when is harassing my boyfriend like an obsessed fangirl no big deal?"

"Um, I wasn't harassing him. I asked him for three signed photos. Calm down."

"Can't you see that Kelsey's using you? She's only talking to Kurt to get access to Ethan."

"No, she's not. She's friends with Kurt. She said she thinks he wants to be exclusive. He just needs a push."

"Have you completely forgotten how horrible she's been to you? And Markita and Ravyne? If you're going to bother Ethan for swag, you could at least do it for people who don't treat you like dirt."

"It's not like that anymore. They're different now."

"Because they're using you!"

"Or maybe they're sorry for how they treated me. People can change."

Can they? Can three girls who've snubbed Georgia every chance they got suddenly want to be friends? Whatever. Everyone wants something from Ethan. Even my friends. Can

I really blame Georgia for wanting the same thing everyone else wants?

"What do you care if Kelsey wants to be friends with me anyway?" Georgia says. "At least she's helping me with Kurt."

"I could talk to Kurt if you want."

"That would be weird."

"Why? If I was having a problem with Ethan and you offered to help me, I'd totally let you."

"Why do you always have to bring the conversation back to Ethan?"

"What?"

"Why is everything always about you and Ethan?"

"It's not."

"Really? Because I've been trying to talk to you forever."

"I've asked you a bunch of times what's wrong. You never told me."

"You're always too busy. Or too obsessed with whatever's going on with Ethan. I never get a chance to really talk to you anymore. Not like we used to."

"I'm sorry. But we're talking now. Tell me what's wrong."

"Why is it that you get the amazing boy and the amazing life and I'm still struggling with Kurt who won't commit? It must be nice not to have problems."

"Of course I have problems. I hardly ever see Ethan anymore. I'm lucky if he picks up when I call."

"That's hardly a problem."

"How can you say that to me? You know it's been hard

having him away all the time. This is my boyfriend we're talking about."

"Yeah, Ethan's your boyfriend, I know. The whole world knows. But the world doesn't revolve around you guys."

"Don't take your jealousy issues out on me. You could have told me what was wrong a million times."

"If you really cared, you'd be making more time for me. The second Ethan started blowing up was when you started ignoring me."

"How have I ignored you?"

"How many times have you canceled plans with me in the past month?"

True, I've had to reschedule hanging out with her a few times. Between going on tour with Ethan and makeup work for school, it's been crazy.

"You're right," I say. "I'm sorry I had to cancel. But it wasn't that I didn't want to see you. You can always talk to me."

"Not really," Georgia says. "Not anymore."

I try to think of what I could say to convince Georgia that I'm still here for her. That I always will be. But too many promises have already been broken. I don't want to risk breaking another one.

31

The security is so fierce at Ethan's Los Angeles show that the bouncer is refusing to let me go backstage.

"I'm on the list," I tell him.

"Sterling?"

"Yeah."

He checks the list again. "Not seeing a Sterling."

"But Ethan put me on the list."

"Why don't you repeat yourself one more time? That'll probably make your name magically appear."

"I'm Ethan's girlfriend."

"You and the twenty-five thousand other girls here. Move aside, miss."

"But—"

"She's with me." Damien swoops in behind me on his way backstage. "She's legit."

No apology from the bouncer. He just lets me pass.

"Thank you," I tell Damien.

"That's guy's a tool. He was even trying to block Zeke."

"How are you feeling?"

"Less stuffy. More drained."

Damien has been fighting a cold. We've talked a few times since I called him last week. Damien is supersweet. When we talk, it's like he's genuinely interested in me. He asks lots of questions about what's going on in my life. I've never met anyone like him. I love talking to him. He always makes me feel better. Even when he's not feeling well.

"Are they giving you any time off?" I say. "You'd get better a lot faster if you could rest."

"Yeah, that's not happening."

"Does Ethan know you're sick?"

"Doesn't matter. Backup roadies aren't part of the package. But one of the guys is mostly covering for me tonight until after the show. I think he felt sorry for me when I drank the drowsy kind of cough syrup by mistake."

Damien walks me to Ethan's dressing room. Drew, Stefan, and Gage are chilling with some friends they invited. Sound check ended a few minutes ago. I don't see Ethan anywhere.

"Where's Ethan?" I ask Drew.

"Wardrobe malfunction. Aixa snatched him away like a ninja in the night."

"Then he has an interview," Gage says.

"Two interviews," Stefan adds. "HBO is doing that backstage behind-the-scenes thing."

"We'll be here the whole time," Gage tells me. "Not being interviewed. In case you were wondering."

The guys look at me. I remember Damien's theory about them looking.

"Want to come hang with me?" Damien asks.

Roaming around backstage was exciting at first. But it can get pretty boring while I'm waiting for Ethan to finish up with the bazillion things he has to do before he can say hi to me for three seconds. When there's nothing to do between sound check and the show, time can really drag.

"Okay," I say.

"Now I don't have a dressing room or anything, but . . ." Damien leads me past the craft service station and crates of equipment to a big, round table. Chairs are haphazardly scattered around. "Welcome to my office."

"I love what you've done with the place. It's very . . . spacious."

"Thanks. I was going for homey but eclectic with a hint of industrial." Damien pulls one of the aluminum chairs out from the table. "Care to sit?"

I sit.

"Would you like a beverage?"

"Beverages, yet. This is almost nicer than flying first-class."

"Almost?"

"They give you warm cookies in first class. And real silverware. And you get as many drinks as you want."

"So? You get as many drinks as you want right here."

"I didn't realize the backstage roadie area was so fancy."

"We learn something new every day."

"Tell me something new about you."

"Like what?"

"Like . . . you never talk about your parents."

"That's the opposite of new. That's old. Old and boring."

"Not to me. I don't know anything about your family."

Damien brings drinks over from a cooler. He sits down right next to me even though there are lots of chairs. "I don't have a family. Technically I have parents. But I don't talk to them. Not since everything shattered three years ago and I moved out."

I wait for Damien to tell me what happened. He just draws patterns in the condensation ring under his can of orange soda. I'm dying to know what happened. What could be so horrible to make someone move out at seventeen?

"Where would you live?" Damien asks me. "If you could live anywhere in the world?"

"I don't know. I haven't traveled much. My mom's been everywhere, though. She tells me about her trips. Europe sounds beautiful. Italy seems like a place I could live. Or Paris."

"What do you like about those places?"

"They sound beautiful. And relaxing. My mom says that when people go out for coffee in Paris, they sit at the table for like two hours. They don't gulp their coffee driving down the street like Americans do."

"We forget to breathe," Damien says.

"Yeah. We really do."

"People are so focused on the next thing. They don't take time to be in the moment."

"The Now."

Damien smiles. "Exactly."

"I can't take credit for the Now. My friend Marisa thought of it."

"She sounds cool."

"She is." I remember how focusing on enjoying the Now helped Marisa deal with her anxiety issues. She's so much calmer this year. She's like a totally different person.

"What were we talking about on the phone last time?" Damien asks. "We were in the middle of something and I had to go."

"Shonda's move." Shonda is Damien's older sister. She just moved into a new apartment.

"Oh, yeah! I wanted to give you more evidence for my higher intelligence theory."

"You don't have to. But I'm listening."

"So check it. Shonda's movers had stacked all of her boxes in the living room in these towering piles. After they left, she was trying to find the boxes with her soap and towels so she could take a shower. One of the boxes on the bottom collapsed and a whole tower of boxes almost came crashing down on her."

"That's crazy."

"She was standing there pushing up against the boxes. She knew she wasn't strong enough to hold them up for much longer. Just when she was thinking she'd have to step aside and let all the boxes fall, her doorbell rang."

"How could she get the door?"

"She couldn't. She yelled that the door was open. And in comes a delivery guy with her new lamp. He could have delivered it anytime that day. But it was at that very second when Shonda needed help the most that he showed up."

"Wow. She was lucky."

"I think there's more to it than luck. Out of all the possible times that day he could have delivered the lamp, he rang Shonda's bell when she desperately needed help. She would have been crushed under those boxes if it weren't for him. I'm telling you. There's some force out there bigger than all of us. Bigger than we could ever imagine."

The possibility of a mysterious force playing us like game pieces blows my mind.

"There's so much more to this life than we know," Damien continues. "There's a lot we know we don't know, but there's so much we don't know we don't know."

"Like when you're thinking about someone and they call you that second?"

"Yes! Stuff like that happens to me so often I don't even think it's weird anymore."

"Or the song you were playing in your head comes on the radio? How can those things be random coincidences?"

Damien leans back in his chair. "You get me. You totally get me."

We look at each other in silence. We don't need to say anything.

The guy who's been covering for Damien comes over to tell us the show's starting in fifteen minutes. I can't believe we've been sitting here for over two hours. Time always zooms by with Damien. Talking to him on the phone for an hour feels like five minutes. Sitting with him here tonight went by in a flash.

Of course I'm excited for Ethan's show. But part of me wishes I could stay and talk to Damien a little longer.

32

Vintage convertible. Top down.

Ethan driving down Cali Route 1. Sterling in the passenger seat, flip-flops pressed against the dash.

Wind in our hair. Radio blasting. Singing along to one of our favorite songs.

We could be filming Ethan's new video. But we're not. This is real life. And I intend to enjoy every second of it.

Ethan was very specific about the kind of car he wanted to rent. He asked Zeke to find a 1953 Corvette Convertible from a private renter. The year was of critical importance. Must be a guy thing. I'd be happy in any convertible.

We're surrounded by remote fields of tall grass. We're completely alone. I haven't seen another car in a long time.

Ethan pulls over into a switchback. "How awesome is this?" he says.

"I know."

"Do you? Do you know how amazing it is to spend time with you alone?" He kisses me. "Let's walk."

We get out of the car. Ethan holds my hand. We walk out into the field. The air is so fresh. Even the temperature is perfect. I can't feel where my skin ends and the air begins.

"It's so quiet," Ethan says. The only sound is wind rustling the willowy tall grass. There are no houses. No cars. Just us.

We find a clearing in the tall grass. When we lie on our backs still holding hands, all we can see are grass and sky.

"This is better than a massage," Ethan says.

"This is better than anything," I say.

"Anything?" Ethan props himself up on one elbow. He slowly leans down to kiss me, his lips lightly touching mine. "Even this?"

"I'm not sure yet."

He kisses me some more. I wish we could stay out here forever.

No screaming fans.

No deranged stalkers.

Just us.

But today is our only chance to do what we want. And there's more we want to do. Eventually we drag ourselves back to the car.

"I don't want to leave," I say.

"We'll be back."

"When?"

"Someday. This is only the beginning."

When Ethan promises that there's so much more to come with us, my worry fades away. I love when he's in a contemplative mood like he is today. On the way to Santa Monica, he fills me in on how his dad's finally accepting the path Ethan's chosen.

"So my dad's admitting he was wrong and I'm like, 'Where was your support when I needed it?' Apologizing doesn't erase all the times he told me I was ruining my life. There were so many times I needed him that he wasn't there for me. And now he wants to act like his lame behavior doesn't matter? Mom was there for me all along. What's Dad's excuse?"

I look out the window to stop myself from saying something stupid like *At least you have a dad*. I know how much his dad's disappointment has hurt Ethan. This isn't about me.

When we get to the Santa Monica Pier, Ethan grabs a bag from the backseat. He takes out sunglasses and a baseball cap. He asked me what I wanted to do today when we were talking after the show last night. I said I wanted to ride the Ferris wheel. So here we are. Ethan puts on his hat and shades before we get out of the car. I put on my oversized black sunglasses.

If I ever live in Los Angeles, I would want to live near the Santa Monica Pier. The energy here is so peaceful. It reminds you to appreciate the little things. The little things are making me happy today. Being here in the warm sunlight at the same time it's freezing back home. Walking on the pier toward the Ferris wheel, holding hands with Ethan, joking about how this one group of seagulls looks like old men.

Then it happens. We're almost at the Ferris wheel. Two girls are walking toward us licking ice-cream cones. One of them looks at Ethan. Her eyes widen. Her mouth opens.

"Oh my god, that's *Ethan Cross!*" she screams to her friend. They start shrieking so loudly everyone on the pier turns to look.

I miss the days when we could go anywhere and do anything. Now Ethan has to hide behind a costume to do the simplest things. And even then he gets found out.

As always, Ethan is good to his fans. He takes pictures with them. The girl who recognized him is shaking so hard she drops her ice-cream cone.

"You were freaking awesome last night!" she raves. "We had seventh-row floor seats. You looked right at me twice!"

"Thanks for being there," Ethan says.

The girls glance at me before going off to post their pictures. That usually happens. Ethan's fans will look at me, but very few of them speak to me directly.

The thing about spotting celebs in LA or New York is that people who live there pretend not to notice. They might turn to stare at someone famous if they pass them on the sidewalk. But they don't run after them for a picture or anything. Fortunately most of the people chilling on the pier seem to be from here. They let me and Ethan go to the Ferris wheel without swarming him.

After a few times around on the Ferris wheel, our car stops right at the top. The ocean extends forever from up here. Sunlight sparkles on the water like glitter. As it did when we were lying in that field of tall grass, time stops just for us.

I breathe it all in. I tell myself to remember how this feels. Ethan. Me. No one else. Here at the top of the world.

33

I really want to talk to Georgia. We haven't talked in forever. But I already left her a message this morning. She's still mad at me. I guess we're officially in a fight. She's been avoiding me at school, she won't return my calls, and she won't respond to my texts.

This has been the most whirlwind week of my life. Flying out to California with Ethan. The show. Sneaking into his connecting room at night. Having yesterday almost all to ourselves. Ethan has a surprise planned for me tonight.

And it's Valentine's Day.

When I woke up this morning and snuck back to my room, I found two boxes on my bed. One was big. The other was a shoe box. They were both wrapped in shiny fuchsia paper with red hearts. The big box had a big red bow. I ripped them open to find the most gorgeous dress and shoes with a note from Ethan saying I should wear them tonight. Ethan told me that he had Aixa buy them for me. She already has jewelry set aside for me on loan from Swarovski. I couldn't believe I'd actually be wearing the pieces she showed me: a beautiful crystal necklace and matching crystal earrings. Which will go perfectly with the crystal-encrusted clutch I'm carrying. It was a gift from Stella McCartney.

Whatever Ethan has planned, it's obviously going to be epic. I've been picturing the two of us alone in some exclusive restaurant he rented out, having the most romantic dinner ever. Then maybe I'd get to go back to the kitchen and meet the executive chef. He'd reveal his most coveted pastry secrets. I cannot freaking wait to find out where we're going.

I take one last look in the mirror before leaving my room. Ethan and I are going down to the lobby together. A limo is waiting to take us to the surprise. My heart races when I think about how good we'll look together.

The dress Aixa selected is exquisite. Aixa is always saying how little and cute I am, how she can dress me up in the most adorable outfits that every girl wants. Tonight I'm rocking superhigh heels and a tiny, floaty dress. Aixa says that super-high heels and tiny, floaty dresses are my signature look. I kind of have to agree. I don't know how she did it, but she's managed to make me shine. The Swarovski necklace and earrings are throwing light everywhere. I'm nervous something will happen to them. How do people accessorize like this every day? Aren't they afraid of ruining such beautiful jewelry?

I knock on our connecting door.

"Come in," Ethan says.

I swing the door open and step into his room. He turns from the mirror to look at me. His mouth drops open. He just stands there, staring. "You look . . ." He comes over to me. "You're the most beautiful girl I've ever seen."

The way Ethan's looking at me, I can tell he really means it. There are tears in his eyes. Which of course makes me want to burst out crying. But it took me half an hour to get my eyeliner perfect. I blink my tears away.

People in the lobby start noticing us the second we emerge from the elevator. Ethan keeps looking at me.

"I can't take my eyes off you," he says.

Melting. In. The lobby.

The limo ride to our mystery destination is ridiculously fun. We blast the music. It's wild how quickly I've gotten used to limos. Now I expect to have the familiar tricked-out amenities waiting for me every time I ride in one. This ride doesn't disappoint with its killer sound system, video screen, and tons of snacks and drinks.

The limo pulls up to a red carpet.

"Surprise," Ethan says.

I look out the window. We're in front of a movie theater. Throngs of fans are screaming.

"What . . . why are we here?" I say.

"This is the surprise. Didn't you say you wanted to go to a movie premiere in LA?"

Yeah. But not on Valentine's Day. Not when all I wanted

was a romantic night alone with my boyfriend.

"Totally." I force a smile. "You're awesome. Thank you."

"I knew you'd love it." Ethan gives me a quick kiss. Then he opens the door.

The screaming gets even louder. Ethan gets out and reaches down for my hand.

Snapsnapsnap! go the paparazzi's flashes.

I'm temporarily blinded after looking directly at an outrageously bright light. A bunch of reporters are filming us. The paparazzi are stacked deep behind the velvet ropes lining the red carpet. I put my hand in Ethan's, swing one leg out of the limo. My four-inch Manolo makes contact with the ground. I propel myself up.

Snapsnapsnap!

We take a few steps onto the red carpet.

"Ethaaaaan! *Ethaaaaaan!* Sterling! To your left! Your *leeeeeeft!*"

I try to look left so whoever is yelling at me can get their picture. The wall of bursting light in front of us makes it impossible to see much of anything. I'm blinded by a thousand flashes.

Snapsnapsnap!

Ethan puts his arm around my waist. I press up against him. We smile and look at the cameras. Fangirls are screaming Ethan's name from behind barriers across the street. We're surrounded by hundreds of people trying to capture this moment, trying to take a piece of Ethan away with them.

Snapsnapsnap!

Ethan kisses my cheek. He's looking at me with the same intensity as before. When he couldn't take his eyes off me. He can't even tell that I'm disappointed.

"Happy Valentine's Day," he says.

34

"Sterling! Hey, *Sterling*!"

I could pretend I don't hear her. I could keep walking from my car to the grocery store. There's a chance she won't follow me in.

"Sterling!"

My body wants to leap into a sprint. But my mind tells me to be careful. There's a serious lack of privacy in my life. You never know who's watching. Who's filming. Who's talking.

I turn around. A girl I recognize from school runs up to me. I think she's a freshman.

"Hey!" she pants. "I was shouting your name!"

Ethan's fans shout my name a lot these days. They approach me all the time with everything ranging from sweet compliments to wildly inappropriate demands. One girl wanted me to sign her back. Another girl came up to me in the drugstore. She would not stop ranting about how she needed to meet Ethan because she swears they were married in a past life. Then there was the crazy stalker who kept following me around the Notch, insisting that I should give her tickets to Ethan's Madison Square Garden show because she's his number one fan. She would not leave me alone. I tried to tell her that I didn't have any extra tickets. She wasn't hearing that. When I asked her to please leave me alone, she got angry. She called me a spoiled bitch who didn't deserve to be with Ethan. It was mad nasty. And those weren't the only encounters I've had with stalker girls. So I'm hesitant about talking to random girls who come up to me.

"Sorry," I say. I don't try making an excuse for not hearing her. They probably heard her three towns over.

"Have you talked to Ethan lately?" she asks.

I nod.

"He's in the Midwest now, right?"

I nod again. He's finishing up the Midwest leg of his tour. Next he has a bunch of shows down south. I don't know why she's bothering to ask me where he is. She probably has Ethan's entire tour schedule memorized.

"Do you miss him?" she asks.

"Of course."

"But you get to see him sometimes, right?"

I start walking toward the grocery store. If she wants to walk and talk, that's cool. Gram and I are cooking dinner at

her house. We're making eggplant parmesan, portobello salad, and garlic bread. We need ingredients.

"Yeah," I say.

"I saw a clip of you guys at that premiere in LA. You looked
so beautiful!"

"Thanks." Photos and videos of us were everywhere right
after the Valentine's Day movie premiere. That was over a
month ago. People are still asking me where I got my dress.

"Where did you get your dress?" she asks.

"Ethan's stylist picked it out. She's amazing."

"OMG *want*. You looked so cute in it."

I smile at her. This girl is harmless. She's obviously nervous talking to me. If she were going to attack me, it would
have happened by now.

We get to the front doors. "Are you going in?" I ask.

"No, we were just leaving. I told my mom to wait."

"It was good talking to you."

"You, too! Say hi to Ethan for me!"

Even though she was sweet, I'm relieved to go into the
grocery store alone. People tend to enjoy scrutinizing what I
buy. Which is hilarious. Why is what I eat remotely interesting? Anyway, it was refreshing to meet a sincere fan who just
wanted to connect with me without asking for anything.

At home, I unpack the groceries. I separate the things I'm
bringing to Gram's house. Then I check Ethan's fan page. Tons
of new comments on our Valentine's Day pics are still coming in. Lots of people said how pretty I looked. Reading those

comments made me feel like less of an impostor. Some of the girls made fan art from our pictures. They added watercolor frames, flowers and hearts, and text like ETHAN + STERLING = TLF. Maybe I should relax more when fans approach me. Most of Ethan's fans really are sweethearts.

I go to the most recent comments on the red carpet video Ethan posted. A new comment has been flagged as spam. I open it.

> Sterling is a nasty bitch. She makes fun of Ethan's fans behind their backs. A source was bowling one night when Sterling and Ethan were there. Sterling was making fun of a girl who got a picture with Ethan. Right in front of her and everything. Who does that? Ethan's fans have been nothing but respectful of his girlfriend out of respect for Ethan. We're supportive of their relationship. We could be a lot worse to her. This is how she thanks us? Nasty. BITCH.

Shock hits me like lightning. I would never make fun of Ethan's fans. That someone would even believe this about me makes me sick. As if the comment wasn't heinous enough, it doesn't have any typos. The person who wrote it seems relatively intelligent.

This sucks. I can't defend myself at all. If I comment back saying I never made fun of anyone, it would look like I'm trying to cover something up. The comment can't be deleted yet, either. I could leave a message asking Ethan to have his on-line guy delete it. But it would take a while for Ethan to pass along the request. He's rehearsing for his show tonight. Even if I get the comment deleted, the girl who wrote it could retaliate harder with something much worse.

Why would someone write that about me? Where does an evil comment like that even come from? I think back to the last time Ethan and I were at Cosmic Bowling. I remember the girl who came up to Ethan. I remember taking their picture. I didn't even say anything to her. Why would some "source" say I made fun of her? How could anyone think I'm so mean?

Then I remember what happened after the girl left. When I was pretending to be an obsessed fangirl. When I was goof-ing off, begging Ethan for a picture. Someone could have seen me and thought I was making fun of that girl. They obviously missed the part where Ethan took a picture of us.

The same picture I have taped to my mirror. The one where I was deluding myself that we could still do normal things, like go bowling.

I examine the picture on my mirror. We look happy in it. That was a really fun night. But now the memory of that night is ruined forever.

I take the picture down. I bury it in my underwear drawer.

35

That horrible comment about how I make fun of Ethan's fans has sparked outrage. It's like every girl who has a problem with me has busted out of hiding in the past two weeks to spew her venom on the world.

"Did you see this one?" I ask Ethan from where I'm stationed on his bed. Reading comments on his fan page. Which I really need to stop doing.

Ethan doesn't look up from his computer. He's been glued to his desk chair all afternoon. He's home for a couple days before his Philly and New York shows. I'm going to both of them.

"Which one?" he asks.

"'My cousin lives in Far Hills. He tried those stupid cookies Sterling sells. They made him retch.'"

Ethan doesn't say anything.

"Or how about this one: 'If Sterling new'—N-E-W—'what was good for her, shed'—not 'she'd'—let Ethan go. Does she really think hez'—H-E-Z—'going to keep a GF who disses his fans?'"

"Not everyone is the typo police," Ethan mumbles.

"What?"

He twists around in his chair to look at me. "So a few comments aren't perfect. Who cares?"

"When half the comments are attacking me? I care."

"There aren't that many about you."

"Have you seen these? Your fans think I'm talking trash about them. Which has devolved into a pile of other lies about me sending them threatening hate texts. I can't believe anyone is stupid enough to believe that. How does that even make sense?"

"They're just rumors," Ethan says. "It will all blow over."

"Unless it doesn't."

"Why are you so bent out of shape? It's not like you to care what other people think. Especially when what they think isn't even true."

"I hate that people think I'd do or say anything mean. Listen to this one. 'I heard S takes pictures of fans at E's shows and talks smack about them after.' Where are they getting this stuff?"

"It's not like you're telling them they're wrong."

"You know I can't do that. But you could."

"Zeke says it's better to stay out of it."

"Do you seriously think it's better to let your fans harass me? All I can do is sit back and watch these skanky fangirls crucify me and it's supposed to be okay?"

Ethan bristles. "Without my fans, I'd be nothing. Why do you always have to attack them? Why can't you be more supportive?"

"After the way they've been treating me?"

"They who? Three people?"

"It's more than three people!"

"No, it just seems that way because you're obsessed with the negative comments. If I cared about all the negative comments I got, I'd hide under a rock and never come out. You have to brush the haters off."

"It's hard to brush the haters off when they're basically forming a club to break us up."

"They would never do that. They respect that we're together."

"You don't think these girls would love to hear we broke up?"

"No."

"Ethan. Every single one of them wants to get with you. If I were out of the picture, they'd feel like they had a chance."

"You make them sound so superficial. Did it ever occur to you that some of them are actually into my music?"

"A lot of people are into your music. You're the only hot artist whose fans range from third graders to grandmas. But a lot of these teen girls are in love with you."

"Which is a bad thing because . . . ?"

"They're irrational. They don't want you to have a girl-friend. They want the possibility of you being their boyfriend. These girls would do anything to be with you. Even if it means tormenting me to get us to break up."

Ethan comes over and leans against the pillows next to me. "That will never happen," he assures me.

"How do you know?"

"Because I love you. I want to be with you. You want to be with me, right?"

"Of course. But it's not that simple."

"Yeah it is. You were there for me from the start. You loved me before anyone knew who I was. That's how I know you love me for me. That proves how loyal you are to me. How much more simple could it be?"

Ethan puts his arm around me, pulling me close. I press my cheek against his chest. His shirt is soft. I breathe in the summertime scent of the fabric softener his mom uses.

"We can be together forever," he says.

I want to believe him. I want to believe that what we have will never change. Now and forever.

36

"Ethan! I love you, *Ethaaaan!*" Girl yelling.

"Take it off!" Someone's mom yelling.

"Go one-on-one with me, Ethan!" Boy yelling.

The yelling is directed at tall gates separating a throng of fans from a private parking lot. The parking lot gives performers and staff access to the venue where Ethan has his Philly show tonight. There are a few cracks in the gate where fans are trying to peek in and yell things at Ethan, who is playing basketball with the band. The basketball hoop Ethan travels with has been set up outside his tour bus.

When the guys first started playing, I was watching them from their side of the gate. Then the gate slowly swung open to let a truck leave. Ethan and the band shooting hoops were revealed. Some fans who were walking from one of the parking lots saw Ethan. They started screaming. Security stopped them from running in. The truck left and the gate swung closed again. Naturally the fans who saw Ethan stayed to freak out. More people coming in from the parking lot caught on to what was happening. Now there's a huge crowd. I went out through a back gate to the public parking lots and came around to the crowd's side. No one's noticing me in my huge sunglasses beyond the edge of the crowd.

"Ethan! I love you, *Ethaaaan!*"

One of the fans nearest to the gate catches a glimpse of Ethan bouncing his basketball close to her. She freaks out. "Oh my god he's right there! He's *right there!*"

A scary security guard is keeping fans a few feet from the gate. There's a green line painted on the pavement. She keeps reminding everyone to stay behind the green line.

A girl in the back of the crowd digs her way to the front. She scrutinizes the scary security guard. When the security guard is looking the other way, the girl takes a tentative step over the green line. Scary Security Guard is on the girl in a flash.

"Do not test me today!" SSG booms. "If you do not step back, you will be dealing with an angrier version of me. You do not want to be dealing with an angrier version of me."

A few girls in front of me have become instant friends. It's awesome how intense experiences like this can bond you for life. They're bragging about how early they got to the *Today* show to stand outside and get a chance to see Ethan before he went in.

"I got there three hours early," says a girl with a pink streak in her hair.

"I got there *four* hours early," tops a girl with a Strand bag.

"How close were you?"

"This close." She pulls out her phone and shows off a picture with Ethan.

"Did Ethan take that?"

"Yeah."

"Oh my god he touched your *phone*?"

Strand Bag smiles smugly.

A girl wearing two *mati* necklaces whips out a CD.

"What is that?" Pink Streak asks.

"A bootleg. Some acoustic stuff Ethan recorded like two years ago."

Scenarios like this are common at Ethan's shows. Some superfan throws down authority when anyone else dares to suggest they have a stronger connection to Ethan. Showing off swag is their way of arguing over who's the number one fan.

"Where did you get it?" Strand Bag demands.

"A used CD place on South Street."

"I'm going to have Ethan sign this again." Pink Streak shows a signed 8-by-10 glossy of Ethan.

"You already met him?" Mati Necklaces freaks.

"No, I won it through his fan club," Pink Streak says.

"You *whore*," Strand Bag seethes.

The gate pops open a few inches. A truck is positioned to drive out.

The crowd goes ballistic.

"Step back!" Scary Security Guard yells.

No one steps back.

"Back behind the green line! *Step. BACK.*" Scary Security Guard's tone has taken on a primal edge.

Everyone steps back.

The gate slowly swings open. The throng of fans restrains itself from stomping over Scary Security Guard and four more security guards lining the other side of the gate in a stampede of passion.

Because there he is. Ethan Cross. Playing basketball in his board shorts and his T-shirt with the old-school speakers that says MUSICIAN for everyone to see.

"I love you, *Ethaaaaaaan*!!!"

"Yo, let me play wit you, E!"

"*I am burning with desire. This will be our night on* fi-YAH!"

I go around to the back gate. Ethan doesn't see me when I pass by and open the stage door. He doesn't know that Damien's waiting for me backstage.

37

A reporter from *The New York Times Magazine* has been following Ethan around since Philly. The reporter is doing a huge cover story on Ethan. He told me that he's most interested in identifying what it is about Ethan and his music that appeals to such a wide audience. I get the feeling he's hoping to discover a secret formula for monumental success.

The formula is obvious. Looks + talent + kindness = massive appeal.

The reporter rode with us on the tour bus from Philly to New York this morning. He'll be at Ethan's Madison Square Garden show tomorrow night. But tonight it's just me and Ethan. Tonight is all ours.

Ethan presses me back against the tinted window. One entire wall of his hotel room is a floor-to-ceiling window with privacy tinting. You can see out, but no one can see in. His room is the penthouse of a boutique hotel. We're on the eleventh floor. High enough for privacy. Low enough to hear the screaming fans outside.

"We love you, Ethan!"

"Come to the window!"

"*Ethaaaan!*"

Ethan slides his fingers through my hair. He kisses my collarbone. My neck. My cheek.

I try to block out the screaming.

"Marry me, Ethan!"

"Come to the window!"

"If they only knew what we were doing," Ethan says.

He kisses me hard. The screaming fans are momentarily drowned out by a police siren.

"Are you sure they can't see in?" I ask.

"Positive. That's the beauty of the blackout feature. Famous people stay in this room all the time and no one ever knows."

Usually no one knows which hotel Ethan is staying at. Zeke always makes reservations under random names. Someone obviously leaked the info this time, though. The hotel warned Zeke that a crowd of fans had already formed earlier this afternoon. People were posting about it online. Zeke offered to put Ethan in a different hotel, but he wanted to stay here.

Now I know why. Ethan thinks this is hot.

He presses up against me. He puts his hands around my waist and pulls me tight against him. He kisses me even harder than before.

This is how Ethan is when he wants me. On fire. The same way he is with everything else he wants.

Of course I want him, too. I want to be more into this. It just doesn't feel like we're alone. It's like all those fans are here in the room with us. And Ethan's two bodyguards are right outside in the hall.

I glance at the door.

"Relax," Ethan says. "No one's coming in." His hands go under my shirt. His kisses get more urgent.

"I love you," he whispers in my ear.

"I love you," I whisper back.

"I LOVE YOU, ETHAN!!!" a fan screams.

"This is too weird," I say. I pull my shirt back down.

"Don't focus on them," Ethan says. "Focus on me."

But I can't. All I can hear is the screaming. Reminding me that I can't even be alone with Ethan when we're alone.

38

It's amazing how, if you're a fan of routine, you can slip so easily into a new routine no matter where you go. I've only been to a few of Ethan's shows and tour life already feels familiar. Staying at insane hotels. All Access passes around my neck. The rush of watching Ethan perform for thousands of fiercely loyal fans. I'm only going to one more show after this. But of course there will be other tours. Lots of other tours.

Tonight is the big Madison Square Garden show. Ethan is surrounded by a million people backstage. His crew is asking him questions and Aixa is holding jackets up for him to choose and everyone is shoving paraphernalia in front of him to sign.

"Ethan!" a gorgeous blonde girl shouts. She has an entourage of three girls with her. The other girls are pretty, but this gorgeous girl blows them away.

"Hey, Marion." Ethan hugs her. Then I make the connection. She's Marion Cross, Ethan's cousin. He told me she'd be getting backstage passes tonight. Ethan waves me over to meet Marion.

"I've heard so much about you," Marion tells me. She's even more gorgeous up close.

"Good to meet you," I say. "You live here, right?"

"Yeah, in the West Village. Do you know that area?"

"Ethan had a show there a while ago. But I want to go back. It's such a beautiful neighborhood."

"It really is." Marion looks around. "Is Damien here?" she asks.

My heart sinks. "You know Damien?"

"Zeke said I could ask for him to show us around. Since this one's too busy for me." Marion indicates Ethan by circling her finger in the air with attitude.

"Sorry that some of us have a show to do," Ethan teases back.

"That's okay. We came to see some hotshot rock star anyway. See you at Christmas, loser." We watch Marion teetering off on her outrageously high platform heels in search of Damien, her entourage trailing behind.

"So that was Marion," Ethan sums up.

"I noticed."

Every guy Marion passes practically breaks his neck to keep watching her for as long as possible. Two stagehands are falling all over themselves to help her with whatever she's asking them.

Normal rules don't apply when you're that gorgeous.

The reporter from *The New York Times Magazine* is lingering at the edge of our thank-you circle to observe. All the key players who work so hard putting Ethan's shows together hold hands in a circle right before every show starts. Ethan says a few motivational words to everyone. They all get psyched for the show. I'm included in the circle, standing next to Ethan.

"This is the Garden," Ethan says to everyone in the circle. "Welcome to the big time. Ladies and gentlemen, we have arrived."

Whoops from the circle.

"I can't thank you enough for everything you guys have been doing to make this tour a success. Liz, you rule for busting my ass every day. You are relentless and magnificent. Zeke, thanks for always having my back, man. Aixa, not only do you make it possible for me to look like a real rock star, wardrobe malfunctions are no match for you. Thanks for your grace and insight. Drew, Stefan, and Gage . . . you're the best band mates I could ever hope for. Thanks for tearing it up like a beast every single time."

Drew and Stefan look excited for the show. But Gage doesn't. The glare of resentment in his eyes is hard to miss. Right before Marion arrived, Ethan and Gage had a huge throwdown in Ethan's dressing room. I was there. I saw the whole thing.

When Gage busted in, I was sitting on the couch trying to resist eating the entire box of Jacques Torres chocolates Ethan's mom had sent.

"Can I talk to you?" Gage asked Ethan.

I got up to go.

"No, stay," Ethan told me. "Whatever Gage has to say, he can say it in front of you."

"Fine," Gage said. "I want to play a bigger role in the band."

"How?"

"You know how. I want some of my songs added to the set list. Maybe just 'Aluminum Rain' to start. Being your backdrop is getting old. I want more cred as a musician."

"And if we don't play your songs?"

"Then I'm out."

I couldn't believe Gage was threatening to leave the band. He plays keys for Ethan Cross. Did he know how many people would kill for that opportunity? The same opportunity he was totally taking for granted?

"Are you really going to let your jealousy spiral out of control so much it kills your career?" Ethan asked.

"My career isn't over. Not by a long shot. I'm just getting started."

"Not if you walk out on us. How do you think a rep as a quitter will benefit your career?"

"People will support me for standing up for what I believe in. I want more for my life than to be a backup nobody. I should be in the spotlight, same as you."

"You could get there if you had a more positive attitude like Drew and Stefan. They'll be successful for years to come. They're loving the attention. You know how many girls want to hook up with them. And you. Why are you acting like no one knows who you are?"

"The number of people who know my name is nothing compared to you."

"Are you going to spend the rest of your life comparing yourself to me? Why isn't what you already have good enough for you?"

"Because it isn't!" Gage yelled. "When guys like you switch band members, most people don't even realize anything changed. Only the most hardcore fans care. Most people don't know my name. And at this rate, they never will."

Ethan shook his head sadly. "I feel for you, man. I really do. But you need to focus on appreciating what you have instead of being miserable about what you don't. You're being set up for life here. What you're building now could make you happy forever."

"No. What *you* have now will make you happy forever. I'll still be living in your shadow."

Since Gage is standing right here in the thank-you circle, I guess he decided not to walk out. Yet. But it leaves a huge question about what's going to happen to the band after this tour ends.

Ethan finishes his thank-you circle speech. "Everyone else . . . you are the ones who make all of this possible. Thank you from the bottom of my heart." He squeezes my hand. "Bring it in."

Everyone stacks their hands in the center of the circle.

Together we chant, "One . . . two . . . three . . . *forever!*"

My seat is at stage left. That's where friends and family sit at the Garden. The performers enter and exit stage left, right in front of the little friends-and-family section. I find my seat. Marion and her friends are sitting next to me.

"Hey!" Marion says when I sit down. "Are you psyched?"

"Totally. Did you find Damien?"

"I did. He's a cutie, huh?"

My heart sinks again. Not sure why that keeps happening. Why should I care if Marion likes Damien?

"He's . . . okay," I say.

"Okay? Oh. Is this like a loyalty-to-Ethan thing? Because you're allowed to think other guys are cute."

I'm trying to come up with a decent response when the lights dim. The crowd screams. Ethan's band comes onstage. Then Ethan comes out.

The crowd goes ballistic.

His fourth song is "Now and Forever." The song he wrote for me. Watching Ethan sing our song to thousands of other girls is kind of heartbreaking. But it's also really cool. No matter how bad my insecurities sometimes make me feel, nothing feels as good as being Ethan's girlfriend.

39

"Hello?" Damien says.

"Hey. It's me."

"Hey."

"Can you talk?"

"Of course. What's up?"

"I have good news and bad news."

"Always lead with the good news."

"I got into the University of Vermont." I just found out. Damien was the first person I wanted to call.

"Sweet! Congrats!"

"Thanks."

"That rules. I'm so psyched for you."

Of course I'm psyched, too. But I should be more psyched. The latest Ethan drama is like a dark cloud hanging over everything.

"Why do I sound more psyched than you?" Damien asks.

"Ready for the bad news?"

"Hit me."

"Did you see that interview with Ethan in *Entertainment Weekly*?"

"No. Why?"

"He said some things that . . . just weren't him."

"Like what?"

"Um, I think the worst quote was, 'I'm a baller now. Money, clothes, girls . . . who wouldn't want my lifestyle?'" Tears spring to my eyes. Whatever happened to always being genuine, no matter what? Whatever happened to his promise that he would always be my Ethan? "I'm worried that *The New York Times Magazine* reporter is going to write an unflattering article."

"Can you call him and defend Ethan?"

"Defend him how? Everything he said is already out there. I can't take it back for him. He can't even do that."

"That sucks."

"Maybe the reporter won't include it. Maybe he didn't even see the interview. He has more than enough material already."

Damien makes a disapproving grunt.

"Sorry I'm like calling you and venting all over the place. I can shut up."

"No, I want to know how you're feeling."

"It's so weird that we're hearing from colleges and Ethan isn't even going." I thought he was in a totally different world when Georgia and I were doing our college apps. But that was nothing compared to how different our worlds are going to be next year.

"Yeah, well. World-famous rock stars don't have to go to college."

"I'm just worried that he's forgetting who he is. Did I tell you he actually pulled the 'Do you know who I am?' line at a restaurant in New York? He wanted to take me to The Waverly Inn the night before the show. It's impossible to get into. You have to make reservations weeks in advance. But Ethan thought they'd let us in because he's Ethan. And they were like, 'I'm sorry, sir, but we physically don't have a free table to give you.' He was mortified. I guess that's why he got obnoxious. But still."

"How are you doing, though?" Damien asks. "I mean, aside from Ethan?"

It's been so long since someone asked about me, I don't even know how to answer.

"Okay. I guess my life has been revolving around Ethan for so long, I kind of forgot to have a life of my own."

"Have you given any more thought to those cooking videos?"

"Sort of. But I've been so swamped with traveling to Ethan's shows and keeping up with his stuff online that I'm crazy behind in school. It'll take me a whole other year to make everything up."

"May I speak freely?"

"Um . . . yes?"

"What I'm hearing is a lot about how Ethan comes first in your life. And I get that. He's your boyfriend and you love him. He's very lucky to be your number one priority. But I'm wondering when you're going to take time for yourself. When do *you* get to be the priority?"

I don't know why I didn't realize this before. But Damien's right. When did my life become all about Ethan? Has it been this way since we started going out? Why did I not notice that my own life was taking a backseat to his?

And what can I do to fix it?

40

I stare at the magazine again. I can't believe what I'm seeing.

There's a picture of me in the style section. Not just any style section. The style section of the leading women's magazine.

Was it really only six months ago when I saw that first picture of me and Ethan in a magazine? I hated how I looked back then. My style has changed so quickly I didn't even realize it was happening.

Aixa has hooked me up with a whole new wardrobe. The pieces Ethan asked her to buy for me combined with gifts of clothes and accessories from designers have resulted in a closet filled with beautiful things. Every time I open my closet door or a dresser drawer, I can't believe I'm in the right room. My wardrobe could belong to any A-list celeb. It's unreal.

Even more unreal? Girls are dressing and accessorizing like me. They're making custom tees that look like the MY BOYFRIEND IS A ROCK STAR tee Ethan gave me, which is sold out. I saw a few links to knockoff tees on Ethan's fan page. Girls are rocking my floaty dress/four-inch heels signature look and posting pics with captions like STERLING STYLE.

This isn't the first picture of me alone to show up in a magazine. Pictures of me with Ethan are everywhere. Sometimes I don't even recognize us anymore. Ethan bought a black Ferrari 250 California Spyder on a whim. It's an extremely rare car that's crazy expensive. He got a tattoo. It's on the inside of his left forearm, right above the bend of his elbow. It says *Forever* in black script. Ethan told me he was thinking of me when he got it. About how I'm his forever.

Except it doesn't feel that way anymore. Right now, I'm planning to be in Vermont for the next four years and trying to accept that Ethan and I will probably see each other even less next year and dealing with the complete absence of privacy in my life. I'm totally stressed out. But for Ethan, it's another night in another city. Another show bringing him one step closer to world domination.

I put the magazine on top of the pile with all the others we've been in. Then I check Ethan's fan page for some major news he told me would probably drop today. There it is. The release date of his second album. With an announcement of his upcoming international tour. There's a new topic being hotly debated by the fans. Ethan was on *The View* yesterday. The hosts were asking him about me. They asked him if it was true that he wrote "Now and Forever" for me. When they asked if Ethan thought we'd be together forever, here's what he said:

"Forever is a long time. I love Sterling. But none of us can guarantee anything forever. Look at the divorce rate. Over half of all marriages end in divorce. No one gets married thinking their marriage will end. But look how frequently it happens."

I'm trying to forget what he said. I'm trying not to think about what it means for our future.

Of course the media is all over this. Rumors that we're breaking up are spreading. Everyone keeps repeating this blurb from the interview:

"Forever is a long time. . . . None of us can guarantee anything forever."

After a few rumors spreading like wildfire and an edited blurb taken out of context being posted everywhere, Ethan's image has gone from beloved sweetheart to reprehensible womanizer. As any dedicated army would, Ethan's fans are defending him en masse. They won't stand for a weak public opinion of their idol. I scroll through the comments on Ethan's fan page. They're also defending his baller slip.

None of them know Ethan. All they've heard are a few twisted blurbs from the media. Did they even watch the entire interview?

What he said was totally taken out of context. They're basing their judgments of him on lies. They don't know.

This is just like when people got all uptight about the baller thing. A person can't be perfect all the time. People make mistakes. Why isn't Ethan allowed to make one mistake? It's so stupid.

I don't know what impresses me more: the fans' fierce loyalty or the lack of typos in their comments. Almost all of them are bringing their grammatical A-game to defend Ethan.

Ethan's calling me. He called me twice yesterday, plus this morning. Nothing like a snarky media frenzy to get your boyfriend to blow up your phone. Right after the interview aired, Ethan called to tell me he was caught off guard by the question. He didn't know they were going to word it like that. But he swore he meant everything he's told me in private.

"How are you holding up?" he asks when I answer.

"Okay."

"I'm sorry this has gotten so absurd. It'll die down soon."

"I know."

"You sure you're okay?"

"Yeah." How ironic is it that Ethan's being more available right when I don't feel like talking to him? Ever since talking to Damien last week when I realized how Ethan-centric my solar system had become, I haven't been as obsessed with staying updated on every little piece of Ethan Cross news. This is the first time I've checked his fan page in a while. I'm not sure how healthy it is to be orbiting Ethan's star anymore.

"How was your day?" he asks.

"Good. I've been working on this idea. For a video series."

"Cool! Zeke will love it."

"No, it's not . . . it's about me."

"Oh."

"You know how I'm into cooking."

"Of course."

"Well, I was thinking it might be fun to do a video series on cooking. Like where I can share my favorite recipes and tips and techniques and stuff. It would probably be mainly geared toward college students. Do you know how hard it is to cook at college? No one cooks unless they live off campus and have their own kitchen. Which I'll focus on, like how to cook on a college-student budget. And I can do some videos on how to cook gourmet meals on a tight budget with only a toaster oven or microwave. I'm not exactly sure yet. I'm still working out the details."

Silence from Ethan's end.

"Hello?" I say. "Are you still there?"

"Don't take this the wrong way. But . . . why would you want to do that?"

My heart sinks. I was really hoping Ethan would be as excited about my idea as I am.

"For fun," I say.

"It sounds more like work."

"But fun work."

"You'd have to plan each video. Film them. Stress over building an audience. Why would you want to put yourself through all that hassle?"

"That's what people do. You of all people should under-stand the process of building something from nothing."

"Why would you want to put so much time and energy into something that would only have a few hundred followers? If that?"

If that? Ethan doesn't even think I could get a few hundred followers? "It's not about how many followers I'd have. It's about creating something. Making a contribution. Connecting with people in a meaningful way. No matter how many people are watching." Doesn't Ethan get that? Where did he go?

"Listen. I'm not trying to be mean. I'm just looking at this on a much larger scale."

So Ethan is basically saying my idea sucks. The first idea I've had in forever that doesn't involve him and he hates it. I can't believe he's not supporting me. I've been his number one fan for so long. Why can't he be the same for me?

I try to remember New Year's Eve. I remember what Ethan said to me. How he said to remember that night when we're apart. To remember how much he loves me.

But that night is from another era when forever meant something. That night is distant. Muted.

Almost like it happened in a dream.

41

"What a squat on you," Gram says.

That's what Gramp used to say when I was little. He taught me how to play cards. Including the game Gram and I always play, Rummy 500. If you have a squat, it means you hold spreads until you can go out. Then you put everything down on the table at once and everyone else has to eat the cards they're holding. I'm not sure how the term "squat" was coined. "Stealth like a ninja" would probably be a better description.

Gram shakes her head at the spreads I just threw down: three queens; the five, six, seven, and eight of hearts; three tens; and four, not three, aces.

"Merciless," she complains. "Just merciless."

"I was taught by the best."

"No argument there." Gram adds up her points and writes down her score. "How'd you do?"

"One forty."

"The squat on her," Gram mumbles. Her pencil reluctant-ly scratches my 140 on the score sheet next to the 30 points she managed to scrape by with.

"You still have a chance to catch up. Sort of."

Gram looks at me.

"What?" I ask.

"I'm proud of you. You're growing into a strong, intelli-gent, beautiful woman. It's remarkable."

"Thanks, Gram." I wonder where that came from. I'm not that good at cards.

Gram collects the cards and shuffles. I notice she's not wearing her wedding ring.

"What happened to your wedding ring?"

"It's being cleaned. So how's Ethan? Where is he tonight?"

"Boston. He's good."

"Such a wonderful boy."

Out of nowhere, I burst into tears.

"My goodness." Gram comes around from her chair on the other side of the coffee table and sits next to me on the couch. "What is it?"

This whole time I've been telling Gram all about the glam-orous parts of being Ethan's girlfriend. About the gloss and shine. About designers sending me fabulous clothes. About how amazing it is to travel with Ethan on tour and watch shows from backstage. I keep the fear and anxiety hidden. Partially because I don't want to bother Gram with the negative side. Partially because I keep hoping the negative side will disappear.

Now I see that it never will.

I tell Gram everything. The nasty fan comments about me. The ways Ethan is changing. How he isn't supporting my goals. How he said he couldn't guarantee that we'll be together forever. I still want to believe him when he promises forever. But it's getting harder every day.

It's so hard being apart from him all the time. Much harder than I thought it would be. Even when I get to see him on the road, it's not the same. It almost feels like what we have isn't real anymore. Somehow our relationship has turned into a spectacle. We're a target for haters. The subject of rumors. A pop-culture debate topic. Will they stay together? Or will Ethan Cross take advantage of his superstar status to trade his high school sweetheart in for an upgrade?

"If you're meant to be together, it will all work out," Gram says. "But if you're unhappy more than you're happy . . . that doesn't sound like much fun, does it?"

"Relationships aren't always fun," I protest.

"No, they're not. They can be downright hard sometimes." Gram rubs my back. "You'll get through this. Just promise me that you'll always be true to yourself. Promise that you'll always follow your heart."

"I promise." I want to follow my heart. I really do. But what if your heart is leading you back to a boy who might not be your forever? What are you supposed to do then?

42

Ethan breaks this news to me on the phone: "I can't go to the prom."

"What?"

"I can't go. I'm really sorry, Sterling. I know how much the prom means to you. I hate disappointing you like this."

There's no way I'm hearing him right. We talked about this. Zeke was going to keep that night free so Ethan could take me to our senior prom. We were supposed to have that final classic high school experience together before it's all over.

"But Zeke said you could go. He knew about the prom before your tour started."

"Yeah, but he kind of forgot about the prom when he booked the Oprah interview. Oprah only does a few select interviews. It was complicated to schedule."

Well. I can't argue with Oprah.

"You're mad," Ethan says. "I totally understand. I suck."

"No, I'm not mad. I'm sad. I was really looking forward to the prom."

"I know. But this interview is important. It'll bring a lot of crossover exposure. Zeke's been working on expanding my twenty-five-to-thirty-four audience."

"I miss you," I say desperately.

"I miss you, too. We'll see each other next week. Then the tour will be over and I'll come home."

"For how long?"

"We don't know yet. I'll be working on the second album all summer. I might have to stay in New York for a while."

My stomach twists. Ethan's been talking about getting an apartment in downtown Manhattan. The thought of him in his fancy New York apartment while I'm three hundred miles away at the University of Vermont is too depressing for words.

When did my boyfriend become just a voice on the phone?

I remember when Georgia and I were talking about how she broke up with Andy back in Oregon before she moved here. She totally did the right thing. Long-distance relationships don't work. Unless you know you'll be together again in the near future. But if it looks like that will never happen, then what's the point?

I want to stay with Ethan. I can't imagine not being with him. He makes me so happy. And I know I make him happy.

Finding someone you not only love, but love being with isn't easy.

There has to be a way to make this work.

"Did you see that fan video for 'Night on Fire'?" Ethan asks.

"No."

"She's actually really good. You should check it out."

After we get off the phone, I go to Ethan's fan page. The fan video was retitled as "Burning with Desire." The still shot of the video shows a pretty blonde girl sitting on a couch with a guitar. I click PLAY.

The fact that this girl wants Ethan isn't surprising. What's surprising is how blatant she is about it.

You're with another girl now
but things change over time.

I can't wait for how
one day you'll be mine.

Watching this pretty blonde girl try to seduce my boyfriend makes me want to call Ethan again. But I've met my allotments of Whiny and Clingy for the day. For the year, actually. I need to stop being that pathetic planet orbiting the Ethan star. I need to focus on my own stuff. Planning the cooking videos. Doing more yoga. Cleaning out my closet. Shifting into college mode.

What I need is an attitude adjustment. I can't let the fear of losing Ethan throw me into a panic. Desperation will only make me less attractive to him. I have to calm down. Be confident. Remember how much he loves me. And hope that he remembers, too.

43

Alone in my room.

On my bed.

Trying to process what Mom just told me.

Gram died.

There was an aneurysm in her brain. It ruptured early this morning in her sleep. She died instantly.

But that doesn't make sense. Gram was fine. She recovered from her surgery. She was back to her normal routine. She felt good.

She was *fine*.

I hate myself for not visiting her enough. I should have visited her more. What excuse do I have? She freaking lives down the street.

Lived.

I can't believe it's true. I can't believe she's gone. The only way this will remotely sink in is to see Gram's empty house for myself.

Normally I'd go in through the back door that opens into the kitchen. Gram would see me out the window over the sink and wave. Then I'd go right in. Gram didn't lock the back door during the day. But there's nothing normal about this visit. This time, the door is locked.

I let myself in with my key. The house is eerily quiet. I want to call out, "Gram?" like I normally would. I want things to be the way they used to be.

I want my gram back.

Everything looks the same. Glasses upside down in the rubber dish drying rack next to the sink. Pillows cheerfully arranged on the couch in the living room. Her desk neat and organized in the den. I sit at her desk. I watched Gram sitting here so many times before. Writing letters. Paying bills. Making to-do lists of tasks that kept repeating themselves over and over, a cycle that would never end.

Until now.

I open the top left drawer. Stationery, envelopes, and stamps used to be in here. Now there's just some kind of legal document, a ring box, and a note.

The note has my name on it.

I take everything out. The legal document turns out to be a copy of Gram's will. Why would she empty out this drawer and . . .

Oh my god.

She knew. She knew about the aneurysm. She knew it could rupture at any second.

Gram knew she was going to die.

My hand shakes as I open the note.

Dear Sterling,

You'll find my wedding ring in the box. The ring is for you. I hope you'll cherish it as I've cherished you these past eighteen years.

By now you've probably figured out that I was ready to go. You might be angry that I didn't tell you. But I wanted us to enjoy the remaining time we had together. I didn't want to worry you. Not knowing when it would happen was the hardest part. There's no way we could have prevented or postponed the inevitable. Please forgive me for wanting us to spend our last days together in peace.

Don't forget your promise to me.

Love,
Gram

A tear drops on Gram's signature, making the ink bleed. I should have been there for her. I should have been over here every day. How could I have let all that Ethan drama get in the way of seeing Gram more?

I call Ethan when I get home. It goes straight to voice mail. I text him to call me as soon as he gets this. My brain is so scrambled I can't even remember if he has a show tonight. If not, he's probably at some important event or photo shoot or doing a meet-and-greet with contest winners. He probably can't get away. Or even look at his phone.

So I call Damien.

"Hey," Damien answers. "How are you?"

"Horrible. My gram died."

"No. I'm so sorry."

I'm trying not to burst out crying. That's the first time I've said it out loud.

Her house was empty. She left me her wedding ring. I said it out loud.

This is real.

"I thought she was doing better," Damien says.

"She was. It happened suddenly."

"I wish I could be there for you."

Damien is not the type of boy I would normally be interested in. The boy who never went to college. The free spirit doing his own thing. No long-term commitments. Not worrying about tomorrow. But he's easy to talk to. We can talk for hours and it feels like a few minutes. He really cares about me. You can hear it in his voice. You can see it in his eyes. And he's always there for me. Which means everything right now.

"Everything will be all right," Damien says. "You're going to be okay."

All it takes is hearing him say that to make me believe it might be true. Damien soothes me in magical ways.

Ethan calls me back a few minutes after I hang up with Damien.

"Why are you blowing up my phone?"

"One call and one text do not constitute 'blowing up.'"

Ethan sighs impatiently. "What's going on? I have three seconds."

"Oh, nothing. Just that Gram died and I thought you might want to know."

"Crap. That sucks."

Awkward silence.

"That's it?" I say. "'That sucks'? Gram is dead, Ethan. Do you have any idea how horrible this is?" The tears I was fighting when I was talking to Damien come flooding out. "You're the one person I wanted to talk to the most and I couldn't even get you. That's so wrong. I really needed you."

Muffled sounds of talking from the other end. Then Ethan comes back on. "Sorry, Zeke had to tell me something. We're sort of dealing with an emergency here."

"Are you seriously talking to someone else when I just told you my grandmother died? What could be more of an emergency than that?"

"The sound system guys—"

"I don't want to hear about it! All I've done is support you and you can't even support me when I need you the most. I've shifted my entire world to revolve around yours. I'm not . . . It's time to shift back to normal."

"What are you saying?"

"We need more of a balance. *I* need more of a balance. I love you and I want to be with you, but our relationship can't be all about you. I'm part of us, too."

"I never said you weren't."

"But you act like I'm not. You used to ask about my life. You used to care about what was going on with me. When's the last time we talked about anything that wasn't directly related to you?"

More muffled talking from Ethan's end. When he comes back on he says, "Sorry, I have to go."

"Did you hear what I just said?"

"Yeah. Look, I know it's crazy right now. Like I told you, things will calm down after the tour. Then we can focus on you. I promise."

"Shouldn't we be focusing on both of us all the time?"

"You're right. But we're in two different worlds. That's just the way it is now. It won't be like this forever."

I can hear Zeke yelling something at Ethan. "Hang on . . . I have to go," Ethan tells me. Maybe he meant to hang up. But I can hear Zeke clearly now.

"Why did you do that?" Zeke yells. "I told you not to be an asshole."

Ethan: "You need to take your control issues for a walk."

Zeke: "You ungrateful brat. I discovered you. You should be more appreciative of everything I've done."

Ethan: "You always make it sound like you're the only one working around here. I've worked hard for where I am. I put years of sweat and blood into this."

Zeke: "Then I came along and made you a star. I work insane hours for you and this is the thanks I get?"

Ethan: "Stop trying to be my dad."

Zeke: "Hey, kid. Your parents aren't on the road with you. I am. You're stuck with me whether you like it or not."

There are muffled sounds from Ethan's end, like he's messing with his phone. Then I hear Zeke say, "We're done here."

I had no idea the tension was this bad between Ethan and Zeke. Of course I knew they fight sometimes. But that sounded horrible. Why hasn't Ethan told me how crazy things have gotten with Zeke? I'm his girlfriend. I'm his best friend. When did I stop being the one person he tells everything to? And what kind of boyfriend can't even soothe his girlfriend after her gram just died?

44

[20,587,113 FOLLOWERS]

Ethan's doing a duet with Taylor Swift. She slinks across the stage to him. All sexy in her skintight dress. Glittery fringe shimmers around her perfectly toned legs.

I can see the glimmer in Ethan's eyes when he looks at her. The glimmer I thought was only in his eyes when he looked at me.

This is the last night of Ethan's tour. I wanted to watch from backstage. I thought it would be more special if I could be closer to Ethan for his last show.

That was before this morning.

Zeke is chatting up some VIPs passing through on a backstage tour. He catches my eye. He smirks, cocking his head in the direction of the stage like *Ethan and his ladies*.

Does Zeke know?

Ethan comes offstage with the band before their encore. He darts to me in a rush of electric energy and adrenaline and sweat. The crowd is going wild for him to come back out.

It's different when I look at him now. When I look at him, all I can see is this morning.

We planned for me to come in this afternoon. But I wanted to surprise him. I couldn't wait to see him again. So I showed up at his hotel room early.

A bodyguard was stationed outside Ethan's suite. He told me I couldn't go in.

Maybe it was the way he said it. Maybe it was the way he couldn't make eye contact. Whatever it was, somehow I knew what was going on behind that door.

Ethan was with someone.

He was with a girl.

Deep down, I knew he was cheating on me. But it wasn't until this morning that I could even admit that terrifying suspicion to myself. It was happening right that second. There was nothing I could do about it. All I could do was perch awkwardly on the way-too-fancy settee outside his suite and wait for it to be over. The relationship quiz Georgia and I took at the gym flashed into my mind. *Which scenario best describes the worst relationship ever? This one. Right here and now.*

Ethan's bodyguard must have alerted him that I was there. When Ethan came out twenty minutes later, he apologized for being on a closed-door conference call. I pretended to believe him. We went out for lunch. I never saw the girl.

"What did you think?" Ethan asks breathlessly. Sweat pours down his face. The last song had some hardcore choreo.

I could confront him. Tell him I know he had a girl in his room. But that would be admitting what's happening. If my world shatters any more than it already has, I don't know how I'll pick up the pieces.

"Awesome," I say. "You were awesome."

Of course this is happening on the last night of the Forever Tour. The irony has not been lost on me. All those promises Ethan made that we'd be together forever were such a joke.

Ethan rushes back out onstage. The crowd goes ballistic.

I get a flash of missing him already.

Like he's already gone.

45

When photos of Ethan kissing another girl go viral, I'm not even surprised.

I knew it. I don't know how I knew it. But I did.

She's pretty. Of course she's pretty. She's blonde and skinny with sharp features. Not curvy like me. Her cheekbones are ridiculous.

People are saying she's a fan.

Everyone knows how much love Ethan has for his fans. Still, I wasn't expecting him to hook up with one. Ethan Cross and Taylor Swift? Totally. Ethan Cross and Random Fangirl? Not so much.

It's weird that I'm not crying. I should be crying. Instead, I'm just numb. I reach for the phone.

Damien picks up right away.

"Hey," he says.

"Have you heard?"

"Yeah. I'm so sorry."

"Who is she?"

"I don't know. Some fan?"

"But how could he hook up with a fan?"

"You know how these girls are."

He's right. Being with the rock star they worship is every fangirl's fantasy. That thing where you're so obsessed with someone famous you think you actually have a chance with them. You really believe that if they just meet you once, that will be all it takes for them to feel the same way about you. That it would be love at first sight. Even if they're the biggest rock star in the world. Even if they already have a girlfriend. It's a fantasy that's never become reality.

Until now.

I wish Damien were here. He can soothe me in a way no one else can.

"Do you want me to come over?" Damien says. He's good at reading my mind.

"Yeah, but . . ."

"But what?"

"Aren't you staying with friends in New York?"

"Exactly. I can drive over."

"That's kind of a long drive."

"Sterling. I'd drive anywhere for you. Don't you know that?"

"Are you sure you're not too busy?"

"Busy waiting around for the next gig to start? It's not until next weekend. What's your address?"

While I'm waiting for Damien to get here, I think about how amazing he is. He's been my rock all along. Listening to me vent about problems with Ethan. Hanging out with me backstage before shows. Sharing his quirky theories and stories with me.

Becoming a good friend when I didn't even realize it was happening.

My phone has been blowing up all morning. Ethan won't stop texting me. Plus he left me a bunch of messages. I refuse to read or listen to anything he has to say. Pictures don't lie. Unlike him.

My heart pounds at the sound of Damien's car pulling into the driveway. Mom is away on a business trip, so it has to be him. I can't believe Damien is really here. That he'll be in my home in a few seconds. In my room.

The doorbell rings.

I take a deep breath. I open the door.

"Hey," Damien says. His eyes crinkle in that warm way when he smiles.

"Hey," I say. I open the door wider to let him in.

"Nice place," he says. "It's so clean."

"Thanks. My mom is into design. Or she tries to be designy. This place is easy to keep clean. It's not like we have a whole house or anything." Why am I rambling like a rambling idiot? "Was it a crazy drive?"

"Not at all."

I want to hug him. I want to say, "I'm so happy you're here." Instead, I say, "Would you like something to drink?"

"Water would be great. Thanks."

We go into the kitchen. I almost trip over a bar stool. It's absurd how jittery I am. There's no reason to be nervous. This is Damien. I've hung out with him a bunch of times. He's always made me feel completely relaxed.

So why is my stomach fluttering with butterflies?

I remember where the glasses are. I get the water pitcher out of the refrigerator. I manage not to drop it. Damien sits at the counter on the stool I almost tripped over.

"You really do love to cook," he says. "All these kitchen toys are awesome. Is that a Calphalon pan set? High-end, girl."

"How do you know they're Calphalon?"

"My mom had the same set."

Damien never talks about his family. I want to ask more about them, but I don't want to stress him out.

I sit across from Damien at the bar. We sip our waters.

"Nice touch." Damien indicates the lime wedge in his water.

"I'm fancy like that. Oh, and the water is infused with lemon and strawberries. So I'm extra fancy."

Damien looks like he's about to say something, but he's trying to find the right words. "How are you doing?" he asks.

"Horrible. It doesn't feel real. Even though I knew it before today."

"You knew?"

"Not for sure. But I had a feeling he was . . . something didn't feel right."

"He's mental to get with anyone else. You can do better. Way better."

"So I've been told."

Our eyes lock. My heart pounds.

"He said we'd always be together," I murmur. "He said I was the most beautiful girl he'd ever seen. How could he say those things if he didn't mean them?"

"They do that. Guys. They say one thing and do another." Damien rubs his hands over his face. "Kill me if I ever turn into my dad."

"What do you mean?"

Damien looks at me. "My dad made the same promises to my mom. Then he started working late. Making excuses for not being around on weekends. My mom thought everything was fine. At least, she acted like she did." Damien rubs his finger up and down the condensation on the side of his glass. "There was this girl at my school. I really liked her. She was a senior when I was a junior. It took me months to get up the courage to ask her out. She came over a few times. My dad was always home when she was over. One night they started talking. My dad's not that funny, but she was laughing at everything he said."

Please tell me this is not going where I think it's going.

"We weren't together that long. If we were ever officially together. She told me she had feelings for someone else. Guess who?"

I shake my head.

"When I found out my dad was cheating on my mom with an eighteen-year-old girl—who I really liked—I knew I could never forgive him."

"That's horrible."

"Oh, it gets worse. My mom took my dad back like nothing happened. She wanted to stay married, like nothing was wrong. Like everything was still the picture-perfect image they'd been fooling their friends with for years. I was disgusted at my dad for cheating with the girl I wanted to be my girlfriend. I was disgusted with my mom for pretending like it never happened. I couldn't live with hypocrites. The life my parents are living is a lie. No way was I going to be a part of that. I just had to get out of there. I dropped out of school. Packed a bag and left. That was three years ago and I've never looked back."

And I thought I was having a bad day. What Damien went through was so much worse. The perspective does make me feel a little better about Ethan. Of course it hurts like hell that he cheated on me. But what's it like to have your husband cheat on you? After all those years together? Damien's mom must have been dying inside.

"I'm so sorry that happened to you," I say. "Do you regret dropping out of school?"

"Not at all. I got my GED on time, so it didn't even matter. I love the freedom to go wherever I want. Life on the road is my jam. Even before everything blew up with my parents, I was thinking there has to be a better way to live. What's the point of settling down when there's so much to see in the world?"

I get that the nomadic lifestyle works for Damien. He seems happy with his decision. But I wonder if anything will ever make him change his mind about having a real home life.

"Sorry for the rambling," Damien says. "This isn't about me."

"No, it helped a lot. Anyway, I'm not as upset as I should be. I mean, I'm upset, but I'm not breaking down crying like I thought I would be. Maybe because I've already dealt with it in a way. Deep down, I knew he was . . ."

"That boy is out of his head. When Drew told me last week, I couldn't believe it."

"Told you what?"

Damien's eyes get big. "He told me about Ethan. About the girl."

"Last *week*?"

He nods.

"You knew Ethan was cheating on me last week and you didn't tell me?"

"I was hoping it was just a rumor. You know how those guys are."

"Yeah, I know how they are. I thought you were different."

"I didn't mean—"

"Do you know I showed up at Ethan's hotel early? When he was in his room with *her*? How could you let me humiliate myself like that?"

"I—"

"What did Drew tell you?"

"He said Ethan was hooking up with some girl. That's it."

"Did he see her?"

"It doesn't matter."

"No, I want to know. What did he say?"

"He said . . . he said she was hot."

"So you heard that Ethan was hooking up with some hot girl before the last show and you didn't bother to tell me? When you knew I'd be at the show?"

Damien reaches across the counter for my hand. I pull away from him.

"Can you go now?" I say.

"Sterling—"

"Just go." I don't want to hear anymore. I thought I could trust Damien. I thought he was the one person who had my back. How could he let me go to that show and smile at everyone on Ethan's crew when they all knew about the other girl? How could he let me be with Ethan that night?

Ethan. Who's calling me. Again.

This time, I pick up.

"Stop calling me," I say. My voice shakes. "Stop texting me. We're done."

"Please listen to me."

"STOP FUCKING CALLING ME!" I scream so loud my throat burns. Then I throw my phone across the room. Let it break to pieces. Just like the rest of my life.

46

The thing about closure is that you can't move on without it.

I would know. I've been not moving on for three weeks. Three weeks of shutting the world out. Three weeks of hardly registering that I graduated and high school is over forever and it's summer vacay and I should be happy.

Three weeks of putting my life on hold.

But life can't be avoided forever. Life is happening right now. And this isn't the life I want to be living.

Georgia said I could come over when I called her this morning. I'm relieved she didn't change her mind about seeing me. There was a moment of paralyzing fear when I rang her doorbell. But then she opened the door and we came up to her room like we were already back to normal.

"New plant?" I inquire about a tall dark green one with yellow stripes along the edges of its leaves.

"Snake plant. He already thinks he owns the joint."

"New plant with attitude."

"That's how we do."

I sit at the end of Georgia's bed. She props herself against the pillows.

"I'm sorry I wasn't there for you," I say. "You needed me and I wasn't listening. I should have been a better friend."

"No. You were living the dream life. Anyone would have gotten swept away."

"Well, that life is over. You don't have to worry about me getting swept away anymore."

"What about Damien?"

"What do you mean?"

"You know what I mean."

I wish I didn't get so flustered every time Damien comes up. I don't want to think about him at all. But somehow, he won't let me forget. He's not calling me or anything. We haven't talked since he left my place. He tried at first, though. I wouldn't pick up or text him back. There was no point. He wasn't honest with me. And after everything he went through with his parents? He should have known that keeping a huge secret from me would never work.

Georgia knows about how Damien stayed with me backstage before shows. She knows about our long talks on the phone, hours that felt like minutes. She knows how much I loved being with him.

She knows. And she knows I know she knows.

"He lied to me," I say.

"Not really."

"Yes, he did. Remember from *Little Black Book*? 'Omissions are betrayals.'"

"True. But he was only trying to protect you."

"If he wanted to protect me, he should have told me about the skank." My face burns just thinking about how many people knew while I was completely oblivious at the last show. Waiting outside Ethan's room while his bodyguard inadvertently threw me pity looks. Holding hands with Ethan in the thank-you circle before the show. Drew was in the circle. So was the rest of the band. Plus all the key players. Every one of them probably knew. None of them told me. But none of them knew me like Damien. He was my friend. He should have been the one to tell me.

"You like the way you feel when you're with him, right?" Georgia says.

"Yeah. I don't know anyone else like him. He's amazing."

"But not amazing enough to be forgiven for one mistake?"

She does have a point.

"What about you?" I counter. "Is Kurt treating you any better?"

"Kurt is history."

"What? What happened?"

"I woke up. You were right. I was so desperate for him to like me. I was settling for someone who treated me badly because I couldn't imagine feeling that way about anyone ever again. But I will. The right boy will adore me from the start. I won't have to convince him to like me. Not that you can convince someone to like you. He'll make it clear that he wants to be with me. I just have to trust that I'll find him."

It makes me so happy that Georgia is respecting herself. It sounds like she understands what I've also just realized.

The right boy doesn't make your stomach twist into anxious knots. He doesn't make you panic when he's not calling. He doesn't make you wonder who he's out with. He fills you with peaceful certainty that your love was meant to be. He will support you no matter what. He's always with you, even when he's not. And you just know he wants to be with you now and forever. Because there's nowhere else he'd rather be.

"How's the video thing going?" Georgia asks.

"Awesome." The day I emerged from the darkness was the day I realized that I have to respect the girl Gram loved. She wouldn't want me wallowing over some boy. She would want me to hold on to my identity.

It was last Sunday. As I'd been doing since the last time I saw Damien, I woke up in a murky depression. I stayed in bed reading without absorbing the story. After scanning the same paragraph four times and still not being able to focus on the words, something snapped. I'd hit rock bottom. There was nowhere to go but up. So I threw back the covers, took a shower, and got ready. Then I filmed my first cooking video without even planning it. Just went into the kitchen and started sharing my top five cooking tips. The comments are really positive. They make me even more confident that I'm creating something that will help others. Unlike when I read the comments on Ethan's page, I'm not afraid of potential negative snark. Negative comments wouldn't shatter me the way the ones on Ethan's page did. That girl is gone. "I'm up to a hundred and twenty-five followers."

"Look at you, all famous. Will you still be friends with me when you're an online star?"

"Fame could never rip us apart. Not again anyway."

"Not even when I'm at Northwestern and you're at the University of Vermont?"

"Not even then."

It's amazing how quickly life can turn around. One minute, you're depressed and convinced that life will suck forever. But then you wake up. You start moving toward your goals. Doors open in unexpected ways. And before you even realize what's happening, your life has meaning again.

47

Marisa and Nash used to hang out on this dock. The summer after tenth grade was really intense for them. I remember how Marisa glowed when she told me about those summer nights here on the dock with Nash, making out under the stars.

Ethan and I won't be making out tonight.

I dangle my legs over the side of the dock while I wait for him. Water reflects sky, a dazzling orange sunset. I watch the river moving. I contemplate how the water is constantly going somewhere, yet it's still right here.

When Ethan walks out to me on the dock, I visualize this as a movie scene. This is the part where the boy comes for the girl. But it's not the kiss at the end of the movie you've been waiting for the whole time.

This is the part where they say goodbye.

"Hey," Ethan says. He sits down next to me.

"Hey."

"Pretty sunset."

Ethan Cross has obviously grown out of this small town. He couldn't possibly be a bigger superstar. Even kicking back in board shorts and his MUSICIAN shirt, he still radiates that magnetic energy famous people do.

"Thanks for seeing me," he says.

"No problem."

"I just wanted a chance to say I'm sorry. And to tell you what happened."

I wasn't ready to listen before. Now I am.

"Hurting you was the last thing I wanted to do," Ethan says. "It killed me that you found out the way you did. I should have told you right when it happened."

"Just to be clear . . . when *what* happened?"

"When I made the stupidest mistake of my life. When I . . . hooked up with that girl."

"That girl? You're not together anymore?"

"Of course not. We were never together. It was only a few stupid times."

"Was she really a fan?"

"Yeah." Ethan laughs. "How amateur is that?"

I watch the water. Flowing forward. Standing still. A lot like the way I learned to be present in yoga. Grounded yet flexible to change.

"You have to know how sorry I am." Ethan touches my

hand. "I am so, so sorry for what I did to you, Sterling. I never meant to hurt you."

"Why did you do it?"

"There's no excuse for my bad behavior." He squeezes my hand. "The worst part is that I threw away everything we had. I miss you."

"I miss you, too." I hate that I miss Ethan. But I do. This whole time I've been struggling to ignore his attempts to communicate. Telling myself he's not worth it. Warning myself against setting us up for the same catastrophic failure. He cheated on me once. How do I know he won't cheat again?

Ethan puts his hand on my cheek, softly turning my face toward his. "Is there a chance for us?"

Part of me is screaming yes. Last summer, I couldn't imagine us not being together. Now here we are a year later. So much has happened. So much we can't take back. It wouldn't work even if I forgave him. Ethan is moving to LA. I'm going to college on the opposite coast. Not seeing him when we were together was excruciating. Being away from the boy you love is pure torture. I can't put myself through that again.

He's looking deep into my eyes. Waiting for my answer.

"I don't think so," I say.

Ethan nods, pulling his hand away from my face. "That makes sense. I'm not good enough for you anyway." He gives me a bittersweet smile. "You deserve much better than me."

This is it. For real. I may never see Ethan again after today.

It blows my mind to think that I may never see Ethan again for the rest of my life.

"Did you see *The New York Times Magazine* article?" he asks.

"Of course." The big Ethan Cross cover story came out a couple weeks ago. Naturally, Ethan looked amazing on the cover. All of the photos inside were gorgeous. Even the candid shots were gorgeous. But what impressed me the most was how perfectly the reporter captured the essence of who Ethan is and the impact he wants to make on the world. I didn't have to worry about negative material wrecking the article. The reporter referred to some rumors and less-than-desirable behavior on Ethan's part, but he focused on the positive side of Ethan's career. Especially why his music appeals to everyone. That focus apparently inspired the title of the article. It was called "Ethan Cross for Everyone."

"Do you remember the last line?" Ethan says.

I laugh. "Oh, yeah. That was classic." The last line was almost like the reporter saw our breakup coming. *Ethan Cross is in the rooms and hearts of so many girls, it's hard to believe he can belong to any one of them.*

We watch the water for a while. Not saying anything. Two people who used to mean everything to each other, sitting side by side in the silence between them.

"Look what I brought." Ethan takes the *mati* out of his pocket. "Too bad my good-luck charm didn't work on the one day I needed it the most."

It's sweet that he felt nervous about seeing me. But this isn't about Ethan anymore. This is about my life and what I'm going to do with it. I have my own lucky charm now. Mom found it in Gram's safety deposit box. It's a butterfly pin with amethyst gems. Gram used to wear it pinned to her scarves when I was little. She would smile when I admired it. I know that's why she left me the pin. She was hoping it would make me smile the same way.

48

Mamaroneck is about halfway between Far Hills and Manhattan. Tonight is their last Summer Nights on the Sound event. They're giving free swing dance lessons. Then everyone gets to dance. It sounded like something Damien might be into. I remember him saying he wanted to learn how to swing dance. So I asked him to meet me there. He's still staying at his friend's place in New York, working at a new venue that's supposed to be the next big hot spot.

I arrive early and find a parking spot. There's supposed to be a vintage red phone booth on the corner. We're meeting in front of it. I find the phone booth. Then I wait, trying not to look as nervous as I feel.

The sight of Damien walking toward me makes my heart flutter. How is he even cuter than I remember?

"Hey," he says.

"Hey," I say.

"You look really pretty."

"Thanks." I tried on seven dresses when I was getting ready. This floaty floral one was the first dress I tried on. Not sure why I was doubting its adorableness.

"I know we're here to dance, but I have to tell you something first. I can't hold it in anymore. Is that okay?"

I nod. It's amazing how after I found closure for myself, everyone around me became motivated to find their own closure. As if we're all connected on a level we can't perceive.

"Not telling you about Ethan was my lame attempt at protecting you. I was seriously hoping it was just a rumor. Or that Ethan would say something to you. I found out like a day before the last show and couldn't stand the thought of not seeing you one last time. Or if I'd told you about the girl and it was true and you ended up taking Ethan back anyway . . . If you wanted to pretend that nothing happened . . . I just couldn't watch. Not when I care about you so much."

Now I feel horrible for not listening to Damien when he tried to explain all this before. He really was trying to protect me. Like when I didn't tell Ethan about the conversation I overheard where Gage was bitching about him. Sometimes we omit information that could potentially hurt a person we care about. Maybe that kind of omission isn't a betrayal. "I'm sorry. I should have—"

"I'm not done."

"You're not? Because of course I forgive you. I'm sorry I didn't give you a chance to explain before."

"Good. But there's more."

"Go for it."

Damien takes a deep breath. "You know I'm a free spirit," he says. "I like doing my own thing. I like not having to be in any one place for too long. Except things are different now. Now that you're in my life."

My pulse races.

"My whole thing was not worrying about tomorrow. But you make me want to see you tomorrow. And all the days after. You make me want to plan a better life. The better life I've been searching for." Damien takes my hands in his. "You're who I've been searching for."

I open my mouth to speak. Nothing comes out. He's literally shocked the words right out of me.

Then I find them. "I'm leaving for college next week."

"I know. The good thing about being a free spirit is having the freedom to go wherever I want. I can move close to you, find a job there. I mean, if you want me to. Burlington has a few decent venues. A friend of mine works at one of them. He said he could hook me up."

"Wow. You've put a lot of thought into this."

"Does that freak you out?"

"No. I guess it should. But it really doesn't."

"You sort of have a preoccupation with 'should.' This life thing isn't about what you *should* do or how you *should* feel.

It's about living for today. Being happy in the Now and trusting that the future will unfold to bring more happiness. It's about following your heart."

That makes me smile. I promised Gram I would always follow my heart. There's no going back now. Moving toward the life I want to be living is the only way to go. A new way of being. With lots of new adventures.

Damien's eyes search mine. "So . . . what do you say?"

"I say . . . I think I need to be alone for a while."

The sparkle goes out of Damien's eyes. I hate that this might hurt him. But I think it's important for me to be on my own so I can define my own life. I *know* it is.

"Not because I don't want to be with you," I explain. "I just need to get to a place where I feel happy and confident with myself. I need to fall in love with my own life before I can fall in love with someone else. When I'm happy with myself, I can make you happy."

"You already make me happy."

"I'm not rejecting you. This is the opposite of rejection. I'm doing what I need to do on my own to build a foundation for a more solid future with you."

Damien nods. He closes the distance between us and presses his forehead against mine. "I hear you. Jumping straight into another relationship probably isn't the best idea."

"Exactly. I don't want you to be my rebound. You mean more to me than that. We have the chemistry and connection. When the timing is right, we'll be together."

"Promise?"

"Promise." I have no problem promising Damien that we'll be together when I'm ready. I know it's a promise I will definitely keep.

Could I even imagine that this is where I'd be a year ago? No way. Still, I know this is right where I belong. Sometimes the life you were meant to live doesn't look the way you thought it would. But it's just what you were looking for.

"So . . . can I see you at all?" Damien asks.

"Absolutely. I'm just not ready for a boyfriend right now. Don't wait for me. Do your thing. We'll both just keep that door open for the possibility of us."

"My door will be wide open for you. Always."

Damien leans down to kiss me. When our lips touch, I know this next chapter of my shiny new life has already been written. Without any typos.

I turn the page.

Acknowledgments

Eternal thanks to Kendra Levin, Regina Hayes, Ken Wright, and all the other friendly neighbors at Penguin Young Readers Group. I am extremely appreciative of your insight, determination, creativity, and wisdom over the past eight years. It has been an honor working with you.

Special thanks to my magnificent agent, Emily van Beek. Your talent, compassion, generosity, and grace are an inspiration to us all. Thank you for dreaming big and believing that we can turn those dreams into reality. You are my angel.

Many thanks to the teachers, librarians, and booksellers who have been such wonderful supporters over the years. You rule for spreading the love.

Glittery thanks to my readers. You are why I write. Thank you so much for making this life possible.

Ultimate thanks to the love of my life, Matt Huntington. After writing eight books about the kind of love I kept hoping to find, I'm so happy you're finally here. I love you. Now and forever.

Jayd Jackson

SUSANE COLASANTI

is the bestselling author of *When It Happens*, *Take Me There*, *Waiting for You*, *Something Like Fate*, *So Much Closer*, *Keep Holding On*, and *All I Need*. Susane has a bachelor's degree from the University of Pennsylvania and a master's degree from New York University. Before becoming a full-time author in 2007, Susane was a high school science teacher for ten years.

You can connect with Susane at:
www.susanecolasanti.com